FINDING LILY

LISA D. ELLIS

SOUL MATE PUBLISHING

New York

FINDING LILY

Copyright©2013

LISA D. ELLIS

Cover Design by Rae Monet, Inc.

Published in the United States of America by
Soul Mate Publishing
P.O. Box 24
Macedon, New York, 14502

ISBN: 978-1-61935-367-1
eBook ISBN: 978-1-61935-163-9

www.SoulMatePublishing.com
The publisher does not have any control over and does not
assume any responsibility for author or third-party Web
sites or their content.

To my children, with love

To Karen, with gratitude

And to Gregg, who finally has to read the entire book!

In memory of my grandmothers and Tina

Like a pearl dropped in red dark wine,
Your pale face sank within my heart,
Not to be mine, yet always mine.
—Trumbull Stickney

Acknowledgements

The idea for Finding Lily was born more than a decade ago, when I discovered my mother, grandmother, and I all shared a fascination for lighthouses. This realization sparked me to wonder what would make a person act on the fantasy to run away and live in one. I was spending a portion of many summers at that time on the tiny Brant Point Beach in Nantucket and the storyline really developed in that beautiful setting.

Writing the book was easy, thanks to the input and support I received from so many friends and family members. Diana Ellis was my first reader and her thoughtful feedback kept me on track. The revisions were harder but also more rewarding, thanks to the support and expertise I received from fellow writer and close friend, Karen Peterson, Ph.D. Working with her made the process a lovely journey and her gift for stringing together words to make them sing continues to inspire me. I am so lucky to have her in my life.

My mother tirelessly edited and proofread the manuscript through every stage, so thank you, thank you, thank you!!!!

Several agents also helped me to make my manuscript more marketable and I am grateful for their input and belief in my work. There are also many other people who contributed to *Finding Lily* and I want to thank them all for their help.

The process to go from manuscript to publication was longer and more challenging than I expected. Marriage, motherhood, career, and the changing publishing world have all slowed down the process, but I am thrilled to finally be able to share Claire's story with a broader audience.

PROLOGUE

The lighthouse is her first true love: each June, Claire holds her breath as the ferry rounds the soft bend in the ocean, and there—looming off in the distance—is the familiar stretch of land that curves like a naked elbow against the dark blue sheet of the water. The lighthouse gleams up from the sand like a beautiful white flower. It's only when she sees the breathtaking sight from her perch on the ferry deck, where she rests her elbows on the slick rail amid people and luggage and noise, that she finds she can breathe again.

Childhood, late 1980s

Claire first met the lighthouse when she was very young, tight in the circle of her mother's arms. She peered over the side of the boat and watched the tiny white ghost of the structure grow and expand into her sight. She felt as if she had willed the lighthouse there. By power of concentration she had made it into the tall, beautiful shape that it was. But even with its height, she sensed it was fragile, like the good china cups she admired from a distance but her mother forbade her to touch.

Surprisingly, Claire's parents *did* let her touch the lighthouse. They were taken aback by her strange fascination for the structure, but not alarmed by it. So when she was about seven years old, they took her to Brandypoint Beach, where the lighthouse sits on a rocky bluff wedged between the sand and the ocean.

From here on the beach, only a few feet away, the lighthouse has the shadows and nuances of a stranger. Claire feels a rush go through her. It fills her up the way she fills her pool toys with air from her lungs, turns the thin plastic tubes into shapes that can float. She feels the same way inside as she sees the lighthouse up close, sees that the base is really a series of white-painted boards. She moves toward them, drawn, wants to explore further.

There's a wooden bridge with long handrails for Claire to grasp onto as she walks in her sandals along the uneven surface, following it right up to the lighthouse. Long, brown strands of grass sway beneath the bridge, but there's no water. She's not very comfortable on the bridge, even with the weight of her mother's hand resting securely against her back. The wooden handrails scratch Claire's palms and rows of sweat drip down the back of her T-shirt. It itches there and she can't reach to scratch. Even though she had wanted to see the lighthouse, now she's beginning to regret it. Her feet feel heavy and slow in the heat, and her head aches. She presses the sore spot with the heel of her hand, willing the pain to go away. Her shadow spreads out long and dark against the lighter wooden planks of the bridge, mimicking her motions.

She imagines that her shadow is a little girl who lives here at this beach and is as lonely for a companion as Claire is herself in the summers. "Hello, shadow girl," she whispers, hoping her parents won't hear her. They yell at her when they hear her having conversations with friends they can't see. Now, she longs for the shadow girl to play with her, to show her around this island. Maybe the shadow girl lives here at night when she's not trailing Claire.

But then her mother interrupts her thoughts. Claire squints into the bright light, following the curve of her mother's hand, and sees a door with pale-green trim that looks like ribbon outlining it. The door is attached to a tiny house that sticks out from the lighthouse.

This marvelous discovery opens up layers of possibilities for Claire. She scurries toward the door, toward the gold-colored doorknob that greets her. Closer, she sees the house has its own little roof above it, like the garage attached to her parents' house. She tries the knob, which is cold in her palm despite the heat, but it doesn't turn. So she settles on resting her hand snugly against the white wall, feels the way it's smooth to the touch even though the paint ripples in spots. She runs her hands up and down the surface; unlike the wall in the schoolyard, this wood doesn't give her splinters.

What she can't see from here, but realizes a few minutes later when she takes a step back, is that there are windows on the side of the house and one above it on the lighthouse tower. These are green-edged, like the door. On top of the structure is a rounded porch with its own pointed roof. Inside snuggles the white light that her father says makes the glow she sees from the boat. Now, she has to tilt her head way back to see it. From this close, the light is dimmer than it appears from the ferry. It moves in slow, steady bursts.

"This is really a house," Claire says, scuffing the thin sole of her sandals against the bridge floor. "Oh, Mommy, Daddy, this is great!" She tugs at the corner of her mother's shirt, grabs her father's warm hand in her own clammy one, wants to share her excitement with them both. "I want to live here," she says. "Please let me stay here! I'll be good!"

"No, Claire, you can't stay," her mother says. "Don't be ridiculous."

"But does anyone live here?" Claire asks.

"I don't know. Doubt it," her father replies. "I don't even know if people still live in these things, these lighthouses, anymore. Can't remember now. They may all be automated."

"Auto . . . what?" Claire can't even remember the word, let alone say it. And what does that have to do with this house? "But don't you think a little girl might live here? Someone like me, maybe?"

"Oh, Claire. Silly! This house is too small for a whole family to live in," her mother says.

"But someone must live here," Claire insists.

"Hush," her father says. "That's enough, Claire." He shakes his head and wipes at the sweat growing on his forehead. Her mother quickly moves in, puts her hand sternly on Claire's back, tries to quiet her.

"It's too hot for all this commotion," her mother warns. She won't even let her try the door again, even though she wants to turn the knob harder this time, to see if anyone will be there.

Claire's father scoops her up in his arms, holding her tight so she can't escape him.

"It's time to go back to the hotel now, anyway," her mother says, cupping the top of Claire's pale hair.

Claire struggles a bit under the weight of her mother's hand and her father's restraint, then she gives up. She's hot and tired. She buries her face against her father's shoulder instead, going very still, crying silently against the warm cotton fabric of his shirt. Her nose runs against it.

"I *will* live there," Claire says determinedly through her tears. "I really will," she swears. "I'll be back, shadow girl. I'll run away and live with you," she whispers into the air. She must, simply must, live in the lighthouse. She just knows it. "I will," she says again softly. But neither of her parents hears her words.

Now, more than twenty-five years later, Claire feels the past unfolding in little wrinkles as the days pass. How ironic that, in fact, she has actually gotten her way and has come to live in the lighthouse.

CLAIRE

Chapter 1

Each afternoon I walk the narrow stretch of the beach, four hundred eighty-one slow steps one way, four hundred fifty-four faster strides back. Occasionally I have to stop to take off my sneakers and empty the fragments of sand that have slipped in right through the canvas. Even so, there are always a few grains that stubbornly cling to the fabric of my socks hours later when I am safely inside the lighthouse. They make a soft, crunching sound against the thick wooden floors. Sometimes I count in my head as I walk along the edge of the ocean. Other times I say the numbers out loud. Counting helps me pass the time; keeping track of all those numbers can be challenging. I walk slowly down, stepping over tangles of seaweed and clusters of broken glass and rocks, going faster on the way back. By then the wind has usually picked up strength and it's getting colder out. The lighthouse tower beckons to me and I rush toward it, taking bigger steps, eager for the security of the building to embrace me and make me warm again.

I first arrived here at the lighthouse several days ago, hoping to try to find some kind of peace—no matter how fragile—to help me survive the recent death of my newborn baby, Lily. She was only hours old when her heart suddenly stopped beating. My own heart wanted to stop, too, in the first few days after she was gone, but unlike Lily's, mine was strong and healthy. A few times I held my pillow tight across my face, burying my nose up against the soft cotton case, trying not to breathe. But inevitably, I would suck the oxygen back into my lungs, my heart pounding stronger, harder, than ever.

"Jim, I think I need to get out of here for a while," I had finally said to my husband, looking around our two-bedroom apartment in Boston, which was filled with reminders of Lily everywhere. They were not only locked into the tangible things, like the stuffed animals and the tiny clothes we had carefully chosen for her, but were also tightly woven into the rugs, the woodwork, and the furniture. I couldn't enter the kitchen without thinking about how I was standing over there, in that corner by the phone, when the nurse called to confirm I was pregnant.

In the bathroom, I could picture myself in the narrow shower stall, big and round, soaping my bulbous stomach, massaging Lily's body with the washcloth, gently stroking the lines of her growing form. And the bedroom brought on the hardest memories of all: when she moved inside me for the very first time and then, nearly half a year later, clutching the comforter cover, surprised and shaking when the contractions grabbed hold. I wanted to leave all this behind, and to also escape from the white, white walls that greeted me when I walked back into the apartment the very first time, only a few miles from the maternity ward and the tiny, motionless body that the doctors said was Lily.

Looking at the sameness of the white paint when I was home made me feel weak and dizzy. Made me feel as I did when I was young and twirled in circles out on the lawn until I collapsed in a heap, too numb to move, while the world continued to rotate around me. Back then, if I lay still long enough, eventually the spinning would recede. Now, though, no matter how still I lay on my bed, there was a heaviness that weighted down my arms and legs. So instead I wanted to get away myself, give myself a break from all of these things that haunted me in ways I couldn't quite explain to Jim.

Jim and I didn't talk about Lily's death directly, of course. We had not spoken of it, except to discuss practical details that needed to be dealt with. Like the funeral service and what to do with the baby clothes we had bought. But otherwise we both stepped carefully around the edges of the horrible "event," so aware of Lily's presence even though she was so glaringly absent. It was strange how Jim and I had existed for so long together without a child and had seemed fine, then all of a sudden we had one for such a short time and just as quickly, she was gone. There seemed to be nothing at all to hold onto afterward. Nothing to join us together in our common sorrow. We each dealt with our pain alone, and this aloneness, at least for me, magnified its strength.

"That's a good idea, getting away. You need a break from all this," Jim said, gesturing to the dining room table where the sympathy cards were still piling up. I couldn't bear to look at them any longer. I had paper cuts on both of my hands from opening so many. It seems the news of death travels like a fire, spreading from one house to the next until everyone we knew—and even people we didn't— was affected by it. Prayers and wishes and nice notes kept coming, long after I wanted to be done with the whole thing and have time to myself, time to grieve. But I wasn't quite sure what grieving meant, or how to go about starting the process, or when it would end.

"Maybe you should go and stay with Sonja for a while," Jim said kindly, glancing at me with the new look he had adopted since Lily's death. "I only wish I could get away from the law firm for a while and go with you." He had a new crease between his eyes and he tried to keep his voice more modulated, as though this evenness could comfort me. Or maybe he was simply too tired to let his voice rise the way it usually did.

The death had taken a toll on him, too, I knew. At night, when he thought I was asleep, he shifted in bed, unable to get comfortable, and his feet, which usually warmed the sheets, now stayed cold as ice like mine always do. During the day Jim showed no real, outward sign of sorrow, but the tension and pain emanated across the new, invisible line that suddenly divided our bed in half.

I thought Jim had a good idea about going to visit Sonja, who's my best friend and former roommate from college. She and her husband Raj live in a nice, boxy house in the suburbs, about twenty minutes away. But they had gone to India for a few weeks to attend Raj's sister's wedding, so that option was out of the question. And Jim's coming *anywhere* with me was out of the question, too. Since Lily's death, he had been busier than ever at work, and most nights he stayed at the law firm until nine or ten o'clock.

"Actually, I have another idea," I told Jim, looking him straight in the face and getting my resolution ready because I knew he was going to tell me I was insane. But I didn't care. Like it or not, I had already decided I was going. "Ida, the woman I told you about who lives in the lighthouse, remember? Well, she offered to let me stay at her place while she's away for a while."

"That's so nice of her," Jim said. "It's amazing how many people have offered to help us out." I knew he wasn't realizing at first that I was actually even considering the idea. I am sure he was thinking, "How could she be?" It was so impractical that he must have figured it wasn't even worthy of discussing seriously. Jim has had more experience with death: both of his parents died when he was young, so I suppose he considers himself an expert on how to cope with this tragedy.

"I mean it, Jim. I want to go—I need to get away from all this, from everyone . . . and everything." I swore I wouldn't lose my temper, even as tears burned my eyes and my voice quivered. I tucked my blond hair smoothly, neatly behind my ears and tried to keep my face calm and even.

"Claire, be reasonable. You're in no state to go off on your own and live in a lighthouse, for God's sake," he said, looking at me as though I had lost my mind. At times he thought I was impractical, perhaps, but he had never thought I was truly crazy before.

"Jim, I've always loved that place. You know that," I said, trying to pacify him.

The veins on the sides of his neck were throbbing with tension as he tried to hold back his frustration and anger. My stomach clenched at the thought that the tall, dark-haired man I had fallen in love with close to ten years ago had suddenly been replaced by this thin, ugly, white-faced stranger.

"Loving it—and living there—are completely different," he said.

"I'm going."

In the past, I might have listened to Jim and let him talk me out of this. I had always looked up to him and respected his clear, rational way of thinking, and I think he was grateful to me for this. When he was a boy, his father had often belittled his ideas, telling him this harshness and constant disapproval would help make him grow up into a strong man. But instead of bolstering Jim up, all it really did was make him dearly crave approval and respect from those close to him. His self-esteem is so tied up in what everyone else—especially me—thinks of him. Until Lily's death, I had always obliged him by stroking his ego and making him feel good about himself and his decisions. I felt, and still do, that our relationship was precariously dependent on this balance of my needing him and his guiding me, and to tip the weight in a different direction could mean our marriage would come tumbling down in pieces around us. I had spent the past four years doing an intricate dance to avoid this very thing. But I was suddenly too sad and too tired to care anymore. I packed my bags to the chorus of Jim's reasons why it wouldn't work.

"It's too far away from here, Claire, and maybe it's not a good idea right now for us to be apart. We should try to deal with this thing together. And you shouldn't be alone anyway in this state—my God, you're barely rational, look at you. What'll you do there all alone during the day? And you know how scared you get at night when you hear noises. You'll be petrified there by yourself, honey. Be reasonable. We can have another child soon. A child to take away some of the pain you feel from losing Lily. I know it's hard to believe now, but someday soon you'll want to have another baby to love and to hold. We both will."

But I kept moving, folding things, putting them into my bag, as though I not only had lost my mind but had also inexplicably gone deaf, too. I pretended I couldn't hear a thing Jim said. But even though I wouldn't respond, his words caused a flicker of pain that seared right through my stomach and up to my chest. It amazed me how Jim could be such a warm, loving man sometimes and so cold and unfeeling at other times. How could he manage to go on day after day as though his heart wasn't breaking? Thinking already about other children we might have when my arms still felt the shape of Lily in them, remembering her softness and her weight and the sound of her cry when she was hungry. And Jim acting as if he was already beyond the grief, as though he was thinking about other children now, conveniently forgetting only a year ago he hadn't even wanted *one* yet; he had said he wasn't ready. But even though I had agreed to follow his timetable, my body had rebelled and before we knew it, I had become pregnant with Lily.

With these thoughts running loudly through my head, it was easy to ignore all of Jim's logical attempts to talk me out of living in the lighthouse. Finally, when he ran out of steam, he gave up. He knew he had lost his case and graciously stepped down from the bench and cut his losses, like the good lawyer he was, ready to focus his energy on another client or another cause, since this one was beyond hope. He had no choice. There was no way he could stop me from going.

"Well, Claire, I guess that's it, then," he said, coming over to pat me lightly, awkwardly, on the arm. Then he disappeared into the bathroom, and I wondered—irrationally, I knew—if he could be crying in there. Jim never cries, but I found myself at times wanting to think that he was.

Now, barely a week later, here I am settled into the quiet of Ida's lighthouse. This island, which bustles with people in the summer season, is deserted and silent in winter, with a handful of year-round residents and the rare weekend visitors who don't mind the bitter chill to the air. In December, there's an annual Christmas Stroll that attracts people from the mainland to come out for a day or two, but other than that, this island will be pretty quiet until the Daffodil Festival in April. That marks the early start of the summer crowds here. I've been spending summers on this island for most of my life, and that's usually when I arrive with the other mainlanders for my first weekend of the year.

Ever since I was a young girl, I've been fascinated by the lighthouse, and spent many warm days on the tiny surrounding beach, daydreaming about what it would be like to actually live there. As I got older, though, my desire to run away and stay here had faded. Yet here I am, somehow hoping the magical feeling this place used to invoke lives on inside me, waiting for me to pull it back up. This beach is also the place where Jim and I first met, so that makes it all the more special to me. In some ways it also makes it easier to feel in touch with Lily now that I'm here.

In fact, since I've arrived, she's found her way into my dreams, filling them up with her presence. Night after night she twists around in my mind like a guppy, slipping effortlessly in and out of imaginary situations that take all of my sleeping concentration to sustain them. The latest dream was the best one while I was in it, yet the most painful one from which to wake. It was about two hours ago I had that dream, but my head and chest still ache from the disappointment of morning, and Lily's inevitable escape.

In the dream, Lily is standing here, but I don't recognize her face. She's grown up to be a little girl, no longer the tiny newborn baby who had died in my arms less than a month ago. Yet I know her right away. She looks about four or five years old, with long yellow ringlets trailing down her delicate back and white skin that looks eerily beautiful against the aqua backdrop of the sky and the sharp greenness of the grass. Her cheeks glow with the same silvery pink cast of my wedding pearls and her eyes flash blue like her father's. (It was his eyes that drew me in when we first met and I'm glad to see my daughter has inherited them.)

"Mommy," she calls. "Mommy—come and get me!" She seems happy to see me, reaching out her thin arms, which sway in the wind like flower stalks, looking soft and boneless. Those arms draw me to her, reeling me in. My eyes burn with tears as they've been doing since the doctor told me she was dead. But this time they're tears of joy, not sorrow, at the idea of holding my baby against me again.

"Here I am, baby. Here I am. Mommy is here."

I race toward her, eager to touch her perfect skin, my hand aching to memorize its smoothness. My legs grow heavy as I near her. Then comes the mean trick. A slim layer of glass cruelly slides into place between us, like a clear fence, that enables me to look but not reach her. The glass won't let me touch Lily.

No! No! I have berated myself since Lily's death that I—her mother—couldn't save her. Again and again I have replayed those last moments in my mind, trying to see if there was some little sign I could have missed that ultimately could have prevented her death. And throughout the long nights lying in bed beside Jim, I've meticulously assessed my life as though there were something I might have done that I'm being punished for now, in this horrible way. But no matter how hard I try, I can't think of anything that could warrant the pain of losing my baby.

Now, I have another chance to save Lily. This time I *will not* fail. I cannot. I must hold my daughter. I *must*.

I claw my fingers through the glass, pulling at the slippery surface, trying to erase its presence. Then it seems to melt away and Lily is near again, just inches away. "Come to Momma," I croon, as my hand connects with hers and a jolt of gratitude flows through me. I've done it. I've gotten my daughter back.

Then sharply, I'm jolted from sleep, transported back to the pale morning light that slides beneath the flimsy plastic shade in the bedroom. The walls are a soft green shade I don't recognize. I realize I'm awake now, and Lily is gone again, and the pain of her death comes with a renewed strength that frightens me. Sadly, I reach out my arms to hug Jim, need his solid weight to comfort me. But my arms move blankly through air. Jim isn't here. I'm alone in the lighthouse in Ida's twin bed.

Chapter 2

The walls of the lighthouse have a dull, mottled surface that's so different from the smooth, glossy white paint that surrounds me in my apartment at home. I study the way the afternoon sunlight streams in through the window and highlights certain spots, etching the surface with the illusion of pools and shadows. Suddenly, these kinds of details have grown in importance. Such painless thoughts provide easy distraction. They keep my mind off Lily. Oops. Lily. I've done it again. All subjects seem to lead back to the one thing I'm trying to ignore.

Lily. Lily. Where are you, my sweet baby? Where is my darling? Lily! Lily!

I glance around the compact room, which serves as the main living area and kitchenette, almost expecting to see her face. But always, I am disappointed. Everything else seems dimmer in the light of her absence. Behind this room is the small bedroom where I sleep, and a bathroom that is surprisingly large—almost as large as mine at home. Different from my apartment, though, are the pictures Ida has hung at intervals around the place. They are mainly stock prints: a countryside, a garden, and a ship. I'm an art teacher in an elementary school and I find such works vaguely disturbing. There is something missing in their executions. But despite their staleness, I do admire the choice of colors. Muted greens, yellows, blues, and gingers. The types of colors I used myself when I painted, an occupation I took very seriously until several years ago. That was before Jim and I got married. Since then my desire to create my own pieces has slipped away. Now I'm content simply to create a life with Jim, something that takes lots of work and compromise. Besides, a host of other things have become more important than my painting ever was.

At the moment, heading the list of importance is the collection of things I've brought with me from Boston. I slipped them out of Jim's dresser drawer, where he left them for "safe keeping," but I doubt he'll even notice they're gone. I have them hidden in the cavernous folds of my purse, protected in a Ziploc bag buried deep beneath my wallet, my lipstick, and a tiny bottle of hairspray.

The plastic bag makes a pop when I pull open the edges, releasing a stream of pent-up air. When the noise stops, I reach my shaking hand in and pull out the tiny identification bracelet first. The hospital clipped the strip of plastic onto Lily's teeny ankle minutes after she was born. What a waste, since after her death, the doctor sliced it right back off again and offered it to me, along with the little cap she wore and the tiny pink knit booties my mother had made for her. I like to run my fingers over the insides of the different surfaces, knowing these things touched Lily's skin. They make her real for me in a way my memories of her can't quite attain. Sometimes I close my eyes and try to find her scent in the pink, knitted strokes. If I concentrate really hard, I can almost feel like she's still here with me.

After a while of holding Lily's things, my head begins to ache. I lie down on Ida's couch and try to relax, but nothing makes me feel better. I can't read or eat or sleep or do anything other than watch the white clock that sits on the end table beside me. Tick, Tick, Tick, the hands say, one more second has passed. The tiny black lines move slowly but consistently, clearly marking the ebbing of time. But even watching this ritual is more than I can stand.

Restlessly, I shift on the couch, kick off the throw pillows with the motion. Once I get up to retrieve them, it seems like too much trouble to sit back down. Instead, I wander out onto the porch, letting the fresh air clear my aching head.

The November wind blows hard, cuts right through my sweater. I prop my chin in my hands and take deep breaths, enjoying the way the sun sets over the island. It turns the sky red, making a sharp contrast against the dark, slick surface of the ocean. The clouds, which were wispy white curls only seconds ago, quickly deepen into purple bruises. Way down the beach, a figure appears, little more than a shadow in the haze. I can't see a face from this distance.

"Hello," I call out. My words get lost in the thunder of the waves hitting against the lighthouse base. "Hello!" I try again, louder, raising my arm to wave.

The person gets nearer, shifting slowly. She's an elderly woman and it appears as though every step pains her. Her left leg drags a little behind her right. She wears an olive-colored parka zipped to her chin and her eyes, which are cupped by heavy folds of skin, look tired in the deepening light. She seems very frail, and the translucent skin on her cheeks and on her bony hands reveals she's wispy thin underneath the heavy layers of the jacket. Even through the weight of the fabric, her shoulders softly shake.

"Well, hello there," she says faintly, her breath coming in little foggy bursts. She comes closer, awkwardly fumbles with the jacket's hood, then loosens it so her coarse gray hair falls down around her shoulders. The strands stand out around her face like a lion's mane. "Who're you?" she asks.

"Claire. I'm staying here."

"Really?" She peers at me, but instead of focusing on my face, her gaze squarely hits my right shoulder. Her eyes are misted over with a faint film, making it unlikely she can actually see me well. Nonetheless, under her scrutiny I'm suddenly overly aware that my eyes are puffy and red and that I haven't even brushed my hair.

"What're you doing here?" she asks suspiciously, clutching onto the bridge railing in front of her. Even though her hands are white maps lined with purple trails, her knuckles stand out large and red from the effort. My own hands ache watching them protrude. "Are you a friend of Ida's kids?" she demands.

"Actually, no. I've never met them. I just know Ida. She asked me to stay here. Watch the place while she's away." I tug at my careless ponytail to tighten it, trying to make it look a little neater. "Who are you?" I ask.

"I'm Sophia. I live over there." She jerks her chin toward a faint line of houses that look far away. I can barely make them out now in the dusk, but I remember seeing them as the taxi pulled in on my way here. They're all big and freshly painted with picket fences and gravel driveways, the kind of homes where people often live year round instead of the more informal cottages on the other side of the island.

"I'm a princess, you know," Sophia says haughtily, moving her hands from the railing to her head, as if to stroke an imaginary crown perched there.

I step back in surprise.

"I'm four hundred years old. Maybe more. I don't remember right now. I'm a little tired from all this talk." Her voice takes on a dreamy quality and she looks past me to the ocean, as though the water is her kingdom. She waves a hand at the sky, makes a tiny bow. But the stiffness of her bones prevents her from bending very deep. Her actions fascinate and scare me at the same time.

When we hear a soft thud from over by the road, followed by the sound of leaves parting, her head bobs back up sharply. Another figure runs over, this one a woman who appears to be younger than I—maybe in her early twenties. She has red cheeks and black curly hair, and looks vibrant and bright against Sophia's faded presence.

"Sophia! There you are. You scared me," the young woman scolds, grasping Sophia's shoulder so the older woman can't escape. "You got away again! I told you not to move." She turns to me. "I'm Diana. I stay with Sophia and take care of her while her children are away."

"Who's Sophia?" the old woman asks harshly. "I am the princess, you know. There's no Sophia here. None at all, young lady."

"Yeah, right, your majesty." Diana says patiently, sighing as she shakes her head at me. "Sometimes she's fine, seems sane as you and me, and then other times, well, forget it. You can't make sense of all her highfalutin ideas! She's always thinking she's someone special. But the truth is, she's Sophia Henderson and she's eighty-five years old. In pretty good physical health, too. But mentally, sometimes she gets delusions. She keeps my hands full, I'll tell you." Diana pauses to take a deep breath, then asks who I am.

"I'm Claire," I explain again. "I'm staying at the lighthouse."

"Hi, Claire," she says. "I hope Sophia didn't bother you too much. She escaped from the house while I was getting dinner for Carlo, my little boy."

"She was fine," I say. "I was enjoying talking to her, anyway."

"Who're you?" Sophia asks. "Where is this place? How did I get here? Take me home this instant. Take me home or I shall scream at the top of my lungs."

"Hush!" Diana says patiently. "Let Claire talk. Claire, how long are you staying here?" She tightens her grip on Sophia as the older woman strains to break away.

"A few weeks, I suppose. I'm not really sure."

"What brings you all the way out here at this time of year?" Diana asks, puzzled, squinting so hard a furrow forms between her eyes.

It's almost dark out, but even in the night sky her eyes shine, a bright blue that stands out against her dark hair and makes her look exotic. I notice that they're almost the same color as Jim's eyes, and this thought sparks a clenching inside me. I imagine him now, back in our apartment, as he settles down on the couch by himself—probably, hopefully, missing me.

"I needed a little rest and Ida was kind enough to let me stay here."

"Are you alone?" Diana moves closer so I can see her better. From the angle where I stand on the bridge several feet above her, I notice dark smudges under her eyes that her makeup doesn't quite cover.

"Yes. My husband stayed in the city. In Boston," I explain. "He has to work. And besides, I needed to be by myself right now."

"I see," Diana says, nodding, as if she knows exactly what I mean. "Sometimes I wish I could take some time away, too. I have no husband. None." Her voice clicks on the word, making it sound like a prayer. "But my son, he's a handful, as is Miss Sophia here. Sometimes it gets to be too much for me," she says. "Now we better go. Carlo, he's only six, and I left him alone in the house. I better get back before he gets into any trouble there."

"Sure," I say, and wave to them both as they leave. The wind is loud but beneath it the sand crunches as Diana and Sophia shuffle off toward the road. The darkness takes the years away, turning their bodies into blurry shapes, so from this distance it's difficult to tell which woman is old and which is young. But then their movements give the secret away. Diana's steps are long and bouncy, Sophia's slow and heavy. I lean my chin on my fist to watch them walk, marveling over how well they match their rhythms to each other. Despite the contrasts, their steps blend into a smooth dance. I watch them go until my eyes ache.

Chapter 3

Every few hours, the ferry horn blows three times, loud, outside my window. That's the warning signal that the boat will soon be pulling into the wharf. At first the noise jarred me, but now I've gotten so used to it, I barely even notice it anymore. Like the hum of the generator that powers the light on top of the tower and the crash of the ocean against the rocks, it's simply something to ignore.

Today, I sit at the kitchen table eating lunch and don't even flinch when it sounds. *Toot. Toot. Toot.* I keep my ears focused on the radio instead, which is my constant companion these days. Right now it's tuned to a soft jazz station I particularly like. I find myself humming along with the pleasant tune, even though it's one I don't recognize.

On the hour, the announcer's voice breaks in, giving the top news capsules. I sit up a little straighter, don't want to miss anything. The stock market is slightly down. There has been a major train derailment but no serious injuries reported. A mother is going to court with her ex-husband in a highly publicized case to fight to keep custody of their daughter. A child has been killed in the wake of gang violence in a California inner city. A little girl, eight years old. She was out riding in the car with her parents. They made a wrong turn and ended up someplace where they shouldn't have been.

The voice of the anchor floats through the room, reading words that, to him, mean nothing. He's not the one who has to go to bed at night and know his child's bed is empty.

I turn off the radio with such force, the knob almost breaks. My hand stings from the motion, and my body shakes.

I came to this lighthouse in an attempt to get away from pain. But even in this sanctuary, it's followed me. Disturbed by the news, I wander around the small living room, pick up throw pillows and books, move and rearrange things. I want to find something to keep me busy. Finally, I'm drawn to a frame on the wall in the corner, which instead of another poster print has an old newspaper clipping centered inside. Curious, I go over to read it. The paper is yellowed and the edges are curled inside the glass, but the type is still clear and dark.

It says:

The Island News, May 12, 1965
Reporting the Truth, Every Day, With Full Accuracy

Lighthouse Saves Men and Reels Them in to Land
by Staff Writer Linda Serriff
Four local men stuck in the wake of a storm out at sea earlier today say it was the Light at Brandypoint Beach that saved them.

The sailors, who were shaken but unharmed when they finally hit land, had been tossed around in their boat in 70-mile-an-hour gales of wind and twenty-foot waves about 10 miles outside of the harbor for close to six hours.

The Merry Men *had been on its way back from a fishing trip to Maine.*

"I thought we were dead," said 54-year-old Roger Charles, who owns the boat and rides the route from Maine to Massachusetts frequently. "The waves were higher than mountains and the other guys and myself, we were almost swallowed up by them. We couldn't see land with all those black clouds everywhere. It was seven a.m. but dark as night." *Charles said the men were all huddled in the center of the boat, praying for a miracle. "I never thought I'd see my wife again. None of us did. Then, Gene suddenly points to this*

flash of light in the sky. We thought we were hallucinating,"
Charles said.

But even as he continued to pray, he turned the boat toward the spot his mate, 47-year-old Gene Callahan, had pointed out. The rest of the crew, 43-year-old John Satty and his 20-year-old son, Pete Satty, all held their breath and waited, fearful of being shipwrecked.

But the men all say more flashes of light came slicing through the sky.

"Then suddenly it was like an invisible force reached out and pulled the boat into the harbor. As we got closer, the light came into view, and it was on the light-tower, and the tower guided us to the shore. It was a miracle if I've ever seen one," the elder Satty explained.

Coast Guard spokesman William Drake said he doesn't believe in miracles, but he can't explain how and why the boat got in safely.

"I've heard other, similar stories about the lighthouse saving people, but I've never seen it for myself. Regardless, that is a bunch of lucky men," Drake said.

I wonder if Ida knows any of the men in the story or if it was the mention of the lighthouse that interested her. And I wonder what it was that had saved the men. There must be a logical explanation for the force they described that pulled them in to land.

While I don't exactly believe in miracles the way some of the islanders do, I have always had a special place in my heart for the Light at Brandypoint Beach. And now I have a special fondness for Ida, too, for letting me stay in her home on this beach.

Dear Ida. I remember the first time we met. It was over the summer, when I was about six months pregnant and taking a bus tour of the island. Ida was narrating the tour. She knew so many interesting facts and I was fascinated by each vivid detail she shared. Even though I had been coming here for years, I had never learned any of the history of the place. But when I was pregnant with Lily, I started thinking more about the roots of things and how they began and I decided to learn as much as I could so as to pass the information down to my baby.

I liked Ida's voice as she pointed out details I had seen but not remembered about the island—like the sterling silver doorknobs and fixtures on a few houses on a small block off Main Street. And the way the cranberry bogs are harvested. And the way some houses—called Shakers—were built when the Quakers lived here, and have a window on only one side of the door and not on the other. Each detail Ida told was so interesting, and I made eye contact with her throughout the tour. I liked the way she smiled at me and the way she seemed to be directing some of her words right to me. Afterward, we talked for a while when the other tourists had left. It turns out she knows my Aunt Gwynn, yet until then Ida and I had never met.

Ida sent me a congratulations card when she heard I had the baby. I think she took a real liking to me that day on the bus. But the horrible thing is she hadn't heard the baby had died. Somehow the news never reached her. I thought she'd sent me a sympathy card when I saw the white envelope with the flower stamp in the corner.

I ripped it open, expecting another note of condolence. But instead of somber flowers or a prayer on the front of the card, this one had a little sketch of a baby in a pink dress with blond hair and a rattle in her hand.

Mr. and Mrs. Edwards,
Congratulations. Wishing you the best.
Your friend, Ida Rowan

She had written the card in her fine, neat script in bright purple ink, which made me smile first, before I cried. The purple was so different from the blue and black pens people had used on all the other cards. It was a silly detail, I realize, but one I've thought a lot about since. I wonder if our other friends would have used lighter, less somber color pens if Lily had lived instead of dying.

After thinking about the ink, the true ramifications of the card then hit me. If I'd had a healthy baby, I would've been wearing the beautiful cream satin bed jacket with lavender and pink roses embroidered on the collar Jim had bought for me, and would've been breastfeeding Lily at strange hours of the night and changing dirty diapers. My breasts still ache with the weight of the unused milk that's stored inside them even now, and sometimes they leak and leave embarrassing stains on the front of my shirts. My mind knows Lily is gone, but I guess my body doesn't.

I don't know what Jim even did with the bed jacket, since it was packed in my new little floral suitcase we brought to the hospital when I went into labor. I haven't seen the suitcase since. Maybe my mom took it. Right after Lily died, Jim bought me a functional navy wool robe to replace the satin one. The wool is so soft it feels like cashmere against my skin. I wear it here at night in the lighthouse sometimes and rub my nose up close against it, trying to find the muskiness of Jim's touch inside the weave of the fabric.

Until I read the card, I think I had been functioning on automatic pilot. Then suddenly the motor that had been moving me along went off at its sight, and all of these things rushed up in me and hit me like a heavy weight pressing on my chest. Then I wept and wept in a new, more violent way than I had so far. The crying scared me with its intensity. My tears were ragged and my breath caught in my chest in painful bursts that threatened to suffocate me, and I wanted to break something or throw something or *do* something that would release some of the tension, but I couldn't stop crying long enough to figure out what, besides Lily's coming back, would help me to feel better. For a second, I did contemplate the idea of ripping the card in half, then in half again, trying to erase it from my mind and pretend I had never seen it, but I couldn't bring myself to do it in the end. I knew it wasn't the answer.

Finally, after I had cried on and on for what felt like hours and raged against the bed with my face squashed helplessly against the pillow, my shoulders began to relax and my chest loosened and I started to breathe more easily. I rolled over then and stared, subdued, at the whiteness of the ceiling, fingering the card in my trembling hands. I decided instead of hating it, I should cherish this memento. After all, it's the only congratulations card we got celebrating the arrival of Lily. This makes it rare and precious: something I'll look back on years later and be grateful to have.

When I was calmer, I finally wrote to Ida to thank her for the nice card and tell her the bad news. Ida was so upset when she got my letter that she called me and apologized profusely. We talked for a few minutes, then I told her how much I've always loved her lighthouse.

"It's such a beautiful place and the little beach is so soothing," I said, picturing the peaceful setting as clearly as if it was right there in front of me. Even in the midst of all of the sympathy cards and my grief, picturing this as I stood there nervously pulling the phone cord around my finger filled me with an instant lessening of tension. For the first time since Lily's death, I had a brief moment when I felt almost like myself again. Then Ida's voice through the phone broke my reverie.

"Dear, I've always felt the same way about this little beach," Ida answered, and I could feel the strength of our connection flowing right through the cable wire that joined us together, bringing her voice from her little island hideaway right into the kitchen of my apartment.

"You must get such a sense of peace waking up there," I said.

"I do," Ida agreed. "I'll really miss this place when I go south next week to see my daughter." Then Ida told me more about her upcoming trip to Florida, how hard it had been to get a flight, how she hadn't seen her daughter in a while. Next thing I knew, she suggested I get away from the city and live in the lighthouse while she's gone for a few months to help take care of it for her. "Ida, thank you, thank you so much. I would love to," I told her, my voice breaking with relief at the thought of finally getting away, as though by leaving my apartment and Jim to live in the lighthouse, I could also leave behind the pain of losing Lily.

Chapter 4

I don't know exactly what it is that attracts me to this lighthouse, but there's something about its strong, rounded edges that has always had a special pull for me. As a young girl, I believe I was overwhelmed by the possibilities inherent in its unusual shape, and in the way the light tower stretches up to the sky, almost like a ladder. But while the lighthouse never actually lifted me to the heavens, I do credit it for bringing Jim to me. Not in the way the men in the news clipping described the lighthouse's powers, but more like a place that brings me good luck or turns old things new again. Maybe like some people wish on the candles on a birthday cake or think something good will happen when they find a shiny penny, head side up.

Jim and I did first meet on this very beach close to ten years ago. Maybe it was meant to be, or maybe it was a random coincidence. I guess it depends on what you tend to believe about such things. Regardless of what our meeting meant, I've noticed in the years that have since passed that the very qualities I first fell in love with about Jim are the same ones now that I want to escape from. In the beginning, I liked the cold, rational side he presented, but now I think it's wrong to be so closed off to emotion the way he is. I spent so much time pursuing Jim, trying to get him to love me back, that I never had time to imagine what it would be like to actually live with him. All of my energy was focused on the chase, and that prevented me from seeing what the catch would feel like when—and if—I was successful in my attempt.

I wonder if all couples experience a similar paradox in their relationships. Being at this beach has brought back many of those overwhelming feelings I first had with Jim, but now they're tinged with all of the things that have since come. Sometimes I wonder if I even still love him any more or if it's simply the memory of the young man he'd been back then that I'm clinging to so desperately. Since Lily died, nothing makes sense any more. Since she isn't here to hold, I hold on to parts of Jim, replaying all of these scenes in my mind, larger than life, trying to find some missing piece that can force everything back into place again.

I was twenty-four and Jim was almost twenty-six during the "summer of Jim," which is what I called it to my friends, who thought I was insane to care so much about a stranger whom I had just met. Now I sit on Ida's bed and stare out the window, remembering that summer day—it was the middle of August—when I caught my very first glimpse of Jim. Right over there, a few feet away from where that seagull had landed. The temperature that day must have been close to ninety degrees. I still remember what a hot summer we had that year, even as I huddle in a blanket in Ida's bed now, trying to stay warm. But if I try hard, I can see the way that the beach looked back then. The day I met Jim there were seagulls, too, poking their beaks in the sand to dig for food.

I remember the sun was shifting its strength over to the other side of the island. I was sitting on the edge of the water, reading, when there was a faint rustle of the dry grass parting. The sound startled me and I turned suddenly and looked up to see a guy, probably about my own age, moving through the thick tangle of grass that separates the beach from the road. He cut through the knotted clusters and came right up to me, rather boldly.

I pushed my sunglasses up on my hair like a headband so I could see him better. The sun was angled behind him, the rays parting to form a splintery outline around him. This phenomenon made him look sort of mystical, like a Greek god. I instantly liked that about him. That, and the way he smiled at me when he got up close. Squinting, I could see that his face was cute but not extraordinary. He had a familiar presence that reminded me of someone I already knew, though for the life of me I couldn't seem to figure out who.

"Hi," he said, holding out his hand to me. It was a nice hand, with neatly tapered fingers and square-cut nails.

I took the hand in my own, noticing how warm and smooth his palm felt against my cooler one.

"I'm Claire," I said.

"Jim. Nice to meet you. Do you live around here?"

"My family rents a summer house about three blocks away. We've been coming here forever. How 'bout you?"

"I'm here with friends for the weekend," he said. "I go to school in Boston but I'm from Michigan really."

"I live in Boston, too. I graduated from the Massachusetts College of Art last year. Where do you go to school?"

"B.C. Law," he said. "I live in Newton." He described an area that was a ten-minute drive from me, near the Boston College law school. He seemed so serious and so straight I wanted to try to make him laugh or sparkle or loosen up. How could anyone be so uptight on such a beautiful day and such a beautiful beach? So I decided to have some harmless fun with him.

"Is this your first time meeting the ocean?" I asked, pushing my sunglasses back down to hide my eyes.

"Huh?"

He had no sunglasses himself and his eyes sparkled brightly. They were a brilliant turquoise color and they almost matched the water. His brow furrowed in obvious confusion.

"The ocean," I said again. With difficulty I pulled my gaze away from those marvelous eyes and waved casually at the expanse of blue that lay before us. A few sailboats skimmed around, creating ripples in the calmness. For a moment, I paused to admire the way the sails billowed out to cup the wind and hold it in place.

"The ocean. Oh yes," he said, nodding his head in apparent relief and scanning his eyes out over the water. "The ocean is sure beautiful."

"But have you met it before?" I asked him again, watching him squirm. He leaned back on his heels and jammed his hands in his pockets, fingering coins as he tried to decide how to answer.

"I'm sorry . . . I don't, I don't understand." He shrugged his shoulders helplessly and blushed.

I liked the way his cheeks turned red. His shoulders looked tense and high, as though he was straining them. I could tell he was a nice young man, and an honest one, who took himself—and life—very seriously. This idea amused me.

"The ocean is a wonderful place to get to know," I said, taking pity on his discomfort. Then I pointed out all the things I could see he was missing: the way the ocean is different shades of blue in different sections, more clear up close and more opaque farther off in the distance, the way parts of the sand are really compilations of tiny rocks that have been ground down into fragments over the decades, and the way the boulders prop up the lighthouse, locking it in place from below like rounded stilts. "I love it here," I added, hugging my knees to my chest and deeply breathing in the moist ocean mist, holding it in my lungs for a moment until they threatened to burst and I was forced to breathe again.

As we talked, I noticed a funny thing about Jim. The more I gestured with my hands, pointing out things like the way the sun framed the lighthouse and made the wood sparkle, and how the waves moved in and out on the beach, in a series of swirls, the closer in he leaned toward me, as though I could see something he couldn't, but he was hungry for me to show him my visions. Really, the things I was saying were so ordinary, laid out there in front of him if only he would take the time to look and see it all for himself, through his own eyes, rather than through mine.

Later, I found out most of Jim's friends were like him and he didn't know anyone as expansive or imaginative as I. It almost seemed like an extravagant luxury to him, I learned finally, that I would spend so much time floating along in my own mind, thinking and dreaming rather than actually doing things. This both attracted him and scared him about me.

That was the beginning of our friendship, which ultimately—way down the road—did lead to marriage. But it took Jim a lot more time and a lot more emotional angst than it took me to realize we were in love with each other.

I figured it out when we ran into each other in Boston on the street a few months later. I was on my way home from work and he was meeting friends in town. I saw him from a distance and thought he looked familiar but I couldn't tell who he was until I got up close and saw the color of his eyes. Those I would remember in my sleep. They were so pretty and so intense and, in fact, I'd caught myself thinking about them, and about Jim, in the time that had passed since the day we met on the beach. I had even wished I could see him again and now here he was in front of me, talking so seriously again about school and the weather and asking about me and how I was doing. Then he suggested we go for a drink sometime and I was pleased. There was something about him—I've never been able to put my finger on exactly what—that was lodged in my mind. But the feeling wasn't mutual, it seemed. We did meet for a drink the following month and we did progress into a friendship, but that was all. He was always careful to keep me at a distance.

It wasn't because he didn't have feelings for me, I later came to understand; it was because he felt too much. He wasn't ready for the intensity of those feelings until he got older. Real love scared him, and still does. I've learned over the years he's more comfortable in situations that make him feel less inside, and therefore don't threaten him.

I lie back on Ida's bed and close my eyes, drifting on these thoughts of the young Jim. Ida's bed is so much smaller than mine—this one is a twin instead of my king-sized one at home—but even this small space seems too empty without Jim.

I stretch out my legs and my toes touch the nubby fabric of the blanket, not Jim. This reminder opens up the empty space inside me even wider. Finally I can't stand the loneliness anymore, so I get up. When I'm standing, at least I don't feel quite so alone. I yank the blanket off the bed and wrap it around me like a cape, then slip on my shoes and go outside and down the length of the bridge to stand on the cold, hard floor of sand and stare at the light flashing in the blackness from the top of the lighthouse tower. It stands out brighter than the tiny flecks of stars and helps to calm me.

The roar of the ocean crashes against the wooden base of the tower and the murmur of the wind moves through the tall grass fringe lining the edge of the beach. The grass is so high it comes up to my waist and the blades sound like the flapping of wings as the wind gently sways them from side to side. Swish, swish, they call. In the cool air, I can almost imagine that the whispering breeze is Lily, softly calling out to me.

It's high tide but there's a hint of seaweed in the air. I stand here for what feels like hours, trying to let my mind float and trying hard not to think about anything. But of course, when I try not to is when I think the most. Images of babies fill my mind and I can't stop imagining the softness of baby skin and the rubbery feel of tiny fingers and toes. How do the tiny crescents of nails get to be so well formed? And the powdery sweetness that seems to seep out of a baby's skin. I can almost smell it in the crisp air out here. My toes go numb and my legs cramp as I let my mind float, and after a while I feel myself getting tired. Then I hobble back inside and snuggle in Ida's bed and let the welcome rush of sleep overtake me.

Sometime in the middle of the night the sound of Lily's crying awakens me. Her high-pitched wail fills the small lighthouse and makes my bed shake with its strength.

I instantly hop up, my feet stinging on the cold tile floor—Ida doesn't have a rug in this tiny bedroom—and pull on the navy robe. Then I rush toward the kitchen area as if to get Lily's bottle before I remember where I am and why I am here.

Chapter 5

Often I think about death and angels, which I feel should really go hand in hand. In fact, many people say at death there's an angel who comes down from the heavens to show the soul the way there. I imagine some folks eagerly embrace the angel and follow its light, joyous to move on to something else, something better. Meanwhile, others tremble in fear at its sight, resisting their path for as long as they can. I wonder if there was an angel who appeared to Lily as she took her last breath. She was such a tiny thing, I'm sure she needed guidance. I'd like to think there are special angels assigned to the babies.

In the tumultuous days when Jim and I were friends and then casually dating on and off, those days before he knew that he loved me, I sometimes likened myself to the angels. I was trying to show him the way to a beautiful future, but for a long, long time he refused to follow me. It probably sounds strange and lofty for me to compare myself to an angel and assume I'm heaven-bound, especially considering the fact that I don't even believe in formal religion. But that's the thought that occasionally would float into my mind at night as I was lying alone in my bed, trying to fall asleep and missing him. Now, even though I think about him a lot, I'm not sure that I really, truly miss him. Yet, when I awaken alone in the silvery darkness of the room, sometimes the tangy scent of his cologne fills my nose as though it has its own presence. That makes me ache to put my hand on his arm the way I often do when he lies beside me.

In those days, this concept about being an angel had less to do with me and how I viewed myself, and more about Jim and why he was putting me through a series of what I liked to call "tests," wanting to be friends but refusing to try a serious relationship with me. Yet I knew by the spark in his eyes when he looked at me, that even though he wouldn't commit, he did love me and would somehow, some way, figure it out. But isn't it ironic that now, several years later, he's the one waiting for *me* -- waiting as I'm all alone on this island, waiting for me to return to him?

I received a letter from him today, on our white parchment stationery with our names embossed in deep blue letters at the top. It was one of our wedding gifts from my parents.

James and Claire Edwards

Dear Claire:

I hope you're doing fine. As I told you SEVERAL times before you left, I really hate you being there, and I hate this letter stuff, but since you turned off the phone there, I am forced to try things your way for a while. Nothing much is new here. I have been bogged down with the Smith case all week, working later than ever and I still can't seem to catch up. But it gives me an excuse to spend as little time as possible alone here in the apartment and keeps me from thinking much. The court date is set for next week but I think it will be postponed. I am still sad about Lily and have been to the cemetery twice since you left last week. There are lots of flowers on the grave from friends and relatives. We're still getting lots of cards, too. I have stacks of them on our dining room table, waiting for your mother to come help me with them on Saturday. The only one I've opened, from Sonja and Raj, I've enclosed in this note. They just returned from India on Tuesday and have been calling, wondering when you are coming home. When are you?

Love, Jim

Sonja and Raj's note is on a plain cream card with nothing on the front:

Claire and Jim—We are so terribly sorry to hear your horrible news. Our prayers are with you in this time of mourning. We wish we had been here when it happened to help provide you with some comfort, no matter how small. Please let us know if there is anything we can do. We will pray for you and hope you will find the strength to help each other get through the pain together. Love, Sonja and Raj

P.S. Claire, please feel welcome to call me ANY time, day or night, if you need to. . . . I am here for you always. S

In the same batch of mail with Jim's letter and Sonja and Raj's note comes a letter from my mother. Hers is written on her favorite stationery, which is a pretty pale green with red and brown birds in the corner. Her address label is stuck on the matching envelope and on the flap is a shiny gold seal, which I have to break to get the letter out.

Dear Claire,

I know this is a rough time for you, dear, but you need to be strong and believe in the Lord's way. Jim needs you now. I was at the apartment this weekend and it was a mess. There were dishes stacked in the sink and Jim looked absolutely AWFUL!!! I haven't seen him look this bad since the week before the wedding when he was so sick with nerves he couldn't eat or sleep. He is unshaven and has circles under his eyes and is getting thin. He says he is fine but I don't believe him. He needs you, Claire, and your place is with your husband. Your father and I wish you would reconsider and go home to him. I'm sure you could be a blessing to each other in this difficult time.

Mom

Claire—Please don't tell your poor mother I've added this piece to the bottom of her letter, but she is WORRIED SICK about you. Maybe you should come home this week. Please think about it.

Signed, Your Father

My mother and father both have a tendency to exaggerate and try to make me feel guilty, so I don't take either of their notes very seriously. I find it hard to believe Jim and my mother aren't doing fine without me. My mother has my father to keep her company, and Jim lived close to thirty years on his own without me, so I'm sure he can survive alone a while longer. It's funny how detached I feel from everyone, even as I hear their voices so clearly in this room.

Just thinking about it now takes me back to the afternoon of the funeral, when everyone was clambering at me then, too, trying to help me in their own awkward ways and really making things worse for me.

After the burial service, we all went back to my parents' house because there wasn't enough room in our apartment to hold all the guests. There were relatives and friends of the family whom I hadn't seen since I was a child. I can't even remember all of them. They all blended together into a mass of black clothes and shiny red faces, all looming over me, clucking and saying sympathetic things, watching to see how I was holding up.

I wished they would all disappear so I could be alone to replay the priest's words in my mind and think about how small and alone Lily had looked lying there in the funeral home, imagine how trapped she must have felt when they closed the lid of the casket. I also wanted to think more about what a pretty baby she was; even in death she looked beautiful.

I had taken a tranquilizer a few hours before and although

it didn't ease the pain, it helped to bend the edges and make me feel like I was watching things from a distance but not actually participating in them.

I sat in my father's recliner by the sliding glass door, which was open a crack, hoping the sliver of fresh air would help clear my head and allow me to make it through the rest of the afternoon without falling apart or, worse yet, fainting. With so many people packed into the room, it was getting too hot. People standing too close to me, touching my hands, trying to make conversation with me. My head clouded at all the noise and my eyes swam, but still the visitors wouldn't leave me alone.

Finally, Jim cleared a path in the crowd and made his way over to me, waving bodies away to give me some room. At first I was grateful to see him. Then a second later, my mood shifted and the sight of him filled me with anger and pain. The negative emotions welled up in a deep, moist cloud in my chest that threatened to explode if I didn't get away. My mouth filled with a sour, metallic taste and I winced, turning my head, trying to take deep breaths of air and force the awful feeling to disappear.

"Honey, are you okay?" he asked, mopping his sweaty forehead with the back of one hand. In the other, he held a plate with a big piece of pastry, already half eaten. The cake glared up at me, gleaming evilly in the light, and a bell went off inside my head. I knew, then, that this cake represented tangible proof of Jim's coldness, his inability to truly love.

"Can I get you anything?" he asked, unaware of my growing wrath. "Aunt Gwynn made some of your favorite strudel." He gestured to his plate, as though I could've missed it.

How in the world could this man be so untouched by Lily's death to stand here eating? I hadn't been able to eat in a few days even though everyone kept pressing food on me.

The sight and smell of it made my stomach clench. But Jim seemed to be attacking the homemade cake with real relish.

I started to cry, or maybe I hadn't really stopped crying since the funeral service and hadn't even realized it. Helplessly, my shoulders started to shake and tears drew warm lines down my face.

Suddenly my mother pushed her way past Jim and gently brushed him aside so she could stand next to me. Silently, she began stroking my hair like she used to years ago, smoothing the long blond strands back from my face and weaving them into a loose-knit braid like I wore when I was a child. I used to braid my dolls' hair in the same way, pretending they were my own babies. Practicing for Lily, though I didn't know it then. This was the way I would have done Lily's hair, if she had lived long enough for it to grow. Would it have been long like mine, and gold and silky? The weight of these thoughts was too much to bear, knowing how I would never see her hair, would never brush her silky strands.

I pulled my head away abruptly, startling my mom, and jumped out of the chair, racing my way through people and furniture and rooms until I got to the bathroom, which luckily was empty. I rushed inside and locked the door, just in time to throw up, my head a dead weight resting against the ceramic rim of the toilet. The familiar chemical scent of the water wafted up to my nose and made me feel both worse and, at the same time, better. My parents, and then Jim, banged on the door, urging me to let them in. But I ignored their pleas and wearily lay my body down on the cold tile floor and cried alone, not wanting this rare moment of solitude to end.

Chapter 6

"Mommy? Where are you? Mommmmmmmmmy."
Off and on over the next few nights, the dreams come to me. Again and again I wake to the sound of Lily's tiny voice calling me. *"Mommy . . . Come and get me, please!"*

But each time she urgently pulls me out of sleep, I open my eyes in the darkened bedroom of the lighthouse and her thin cry is swallowed up by the louder, harsher noises of the beach. Then I lie there, pressing my shoulder tight into the mattress, cradling my knees up to my chest, trying to fill the empty space that opens up inside of me. Sometimes I wish that Jim, or my mother, were here. Other times, I'm glad I'm alone. In the darkness of the room, I think about what it would be like to disappear here forever.

In the mornings, my body feels battered and tense. I drag myself to the kitchen for some hot tea, then back to the bed, where I stay very still in the darkened room, keeping the shades drawn for as long as I can bear it. Much of the time I don't have the energy or inclination to dress, preferring the loose comfort of my big nightshirt to the stiffness of clothes. When I get bored, I turn on the bedside lamp, which casts barely enough light to read the fine print of the books I'd brought with me. There are four of them, all slim volumes with pretty covers. One depicts an endless ocean view, another a green meadow dotted with wildflowers, the third is of the cloudless blue sky with the faint outline of birds and the last one is a close-up of delicate arrangement of lavender flowers atop a cherry table. Despite their different photographs, though, they all seem vaguely similar. Absently I flip through the dry pages, enjoying the way the surface lays out crisp and new beneath my fingertips. The words inside each book are all about grief and loss and coping. They contain paragraph after paragraph of wisdom, yet none of it seems to make me feel any better.

In the afternoons, I get restless. I force myself to get up; my joints creak from the motion, and I pull on my sweat pants and one of Jim's faded tee shirts. Then I meander into the living room and press my forehead against the smoothness of the windowpanes, watching the sun's daily descent. I love the moment when the deepening gray lowers itself like a bride's veil to soften the harshness of afternoon light.

Today the onset of dusk feels comforting at first, but after a few moments, the unfamiliar shapes in the room take on menacing casts. Abruptly I switch on the lamp and break the eerie mood as the room is suddenly flooded in brightness.

Then I go into the kitchen to make myself a cup of tea. As I pour the steaming water into a china cup, I hear a soft thud. Startled, I look around the small room, wondering if a board has come loose from the outside wall. When the sound comes again, though, I realize it's someone knocking. This is the first time since I've arrived that anyone has come to visit me and I'm slightly nervous when I go to the door.

"Hello?" I peer outside, welcoming the soft rush of air that strokes my face.

There's a little boy standing on the bridge, looking up at me. He has a burst of thick curls that form a fringe on his forehead and shiny blue eyes. Instantly I'm reminded of that young woman, Diana, I met the other night. This must be her son. She said his name was Carlo, I think. I doubt there are many children here at this time of year, especially wandering around alone. He looks too young to be out by himself, though. He barely comes up to my waist.

"Lady?" he says. "Can I come in?"

"Carlo?"

"How do you know me?" he asks, taking a step away.

"I met Diana, I mean your mom, the other night."

"You know my momma?" he asks.

"Yep. Where is she, anyway? She doesn't let you out alone, does she?" I scan the darkening beach, searching for a sign of Diana, but no one else seems to be around.

"I'm a big boy! I'm six!" Carlo stands up straighter, putting his small fists on his hips as if to prove his maturity. "I know my own way!"

"Still, you shouldn't be wandering alone like this." I place my hand on top of Carlo's small head, and am surprised by the softness of his hair beneath my palm. I thought the curls would be rougher than this. There's a faint smell of shampoo wafting up and I take a deep breath, letting the meadow-fresh scent drift through me. He wears a blue jacket, unzipped, with a white cotton shirt and jeans, and his chest moves up and down, in slight, even lines, the way a child's breathing should be. Carlo is so vibrant and alive. A sharp pain shoots through my stomach, startling me with its strength, and I'm aware of the weight of my breasts and the way the area between my legs still vaguely aches from the strain of the labor.

"Carlo, you need to go home. You're too young to be out alone. I'm sure your mom must be so worried about you."

"No, ma'am. She don't care. She's busy with the old lady. You got any food? I'm hunnnngry."

"Well. . ." I look at Carlo, then down the beach,

wondering where in the world his mother is. "It's almost dinnertime. I'm sure your mom is waiting for you."

"We don't eat till late," he says.

"Hmmm, I guess I'll get you a snack, then take you home. Your mom will be worried about you, so we better make it quick."

"My momma knows I'm a big boy. She even said so last night."

"Sure you are, honey. Come on in and have some food, then you can show me where you live."

Carlo darts into the lighthouse, then stops short. His eyes grow wide as he looks around the room.

"Nice place," he says. "I like it a lot."

"Thanks. Haven't you ever been here before?"

"Nahhhhh. The light lady, she don't let kids in her place. She says no one can come inside. But I wanted to see this place. Where's the room with the light? I thought it would be here." He looks down at his Nike sneakers sadly, and I can feel the strength of his disappointment wafting through me. I remember, then, when I was his age, and how badly I had wanted to see the inside of the lighthouse, too.

"That's actually in the other building, which is attached to the house. It's on the other side of the wall." I point to the door separating the house from the tower, looking at Carlo to see if he understands.

He nods. "The light is beautiful," he says, smiling at me. "I like to watch it sometimes."

"I do, too. Sometimes, when I can't sleep, I go outside and watch it in the dark. I've loved it since I was about your age, too."

Carlo scurries around the compact house, touching everything with his hands, resting his cheek against the couch, the table, the wall, as though he's memorizing what everything feels like.

I find an unopened jar of peanut butter in the cabinet and make him a sandwich and pour him some juice. Then I sit down at the table with him. His thin legs wrap around the chair rungs for support, and his chin barely comes up above the table. He has to stretch his arms up to reach his plate, but this doesn't seem to bother him. It's so nice sitting here, with this little boy. He munches his sandwich and doesn't speak, yet I feel a warmth toward him I haven't experienced in a while. The tightness in my chests relaxes slightly. I sip my tea and enjoy the silence.

"Lady," Carlo says, when his sandwich is done, "why you sad?" He rubs his hands across his mouth to sweep away the lingering crumbs.

"Sad? What do you mean?" I know children are intuitive, but I can't imagine I've said or done anything that would give Carlo this information today.

"Momma and the old lady, they talk about you and say you sad. They said something very bad happened." Carlo peers at me from beneath his long lashes, waiting to see how I'll take his words.

"Oh." I glance down at the tabletop, then back at his face. News travels fast, I guess, even somewhere this remote. "Well, something sad did happen." I pause for a minute, measuring my words. I'm unsure what you tell children in a situation like this. I don't want to upset him, after all. On the other hand, I remember when I was a child, I liked people to be straight with me. Because of that, I decide to tell him the truth. "Honey, I had a baby and she died. I miss her very, very much."

Carlo thinks about what I've said for a minute, then he climbs down from his chair and comes over to me and stands very still, watching me. "Lady, you can share me. My momma won't mind. Don't be sad."

He reaches up his tiny arms and gives me a sweet, strong hug.

I hug him back, tears stinging my eyes, marveling over the strength and compassion of children and wondering what my own daughter would have been like.

After I put the dishes in the sink, I take Carlo home. The boy holds my hand as we walk silently down the beach, leading the way to the house where he and his mother live with Sophia.

The house is a white Cape Cod, set back a bit from the road. There's a chipped white fence in front and lights glowing from several windows. Diana comes rushing to the door as soon as we approach.

"Carlo, you scared me to death," she says, running out to give the boy a big hug, then stepping back to scold him. "What did I tell you, young man, about wandering off on your own!"

"I went to visit the sad lady, Momma. You said she was lonely! She gave me a sandwich, and juice, too. It was yummy. Don't be mad!"

Diana shakes her head and ushers Carlo through the door, giving him a light swipe on his bottom as he passes her. I follow him inside.

I had expected the house to be soft and comfortable inside, like most of the houses on the island. But this one bristles with its formality, surprising me, making me curious about how an active child like Carlo can stand his surroundings. There are stiff-backed velvet chairs in shades of dark burgundy and china dolls with glass eyes on countertops and lining the shelves of the big wooden open-faced cabinets. The place reminds me of an old museum where you're afraid of getting lost inside its deep folds. I shiver, wondering what in the world had possessed Sophia to decorate like this.

The living room, which spreads out from the hallway, is the worst. Dolls are everywhere and I turn, slowly, trying to feel at ease in the gloominess of the room. A long, lace runner spans the length of the coffee table, with another on the couch back. I can't imagine anyone could really sit here surrounded by all of this heaviness. Even the curtains, a crocheted cream lace, look thick and forbidding at the windows, as if they're deliberately placed there to stand guard during the day and keep any light from entering.

Diana smiles as I take in the surroundings, reading my bewilderment clearly.

"I know. It's terrible," she says. "This place gives me the creeps, too. It feels like a mausoleum, but Sophia won't let me touch anything, except to clean. It all collects dust like you wouldn't believe!"

I shake my head at her words, then suddenly feel someone staring at me. I turn abruptly, wondering who else is there, jumping when I realize it's a doll, perched on a chair, her long hair trailing over the shoulders of her green dress with a perfect lace collar. Her cheeks are painted with red circles and she has long, dark lashes. Carlo runs over to the doll and sticks his tongue out at her, then giggles as his mother makes a mad face at him.

"Go up to your room now and change," she tells him sharply. She turns to me, her tone growing warmer.

"Claire, thanks so much for bringing him home. He's so headstrong for such a small child. I can't seem to control him. Sorry if he bothered you. First Sophia, now Carlo. You need your peace and we don't leave you alone."

"I enjoyed Carlo's visit very much! He's a great boy. You're very lucky."

"I know." Diana clutches her hands near her heart. "I am lucky, only I worry about him so much, always sneaking off when my back is turned. He's at that age for exploring, and he's lonely here, with no other kids around this time of year." She shakes her head and shrugs. "Ay, but what can y' do?"

We hear the thud of Carlo's sneakers as he runs through the house. A few seconds later there's a loud crash, followed by the tinkle of glass hitting the floor, then Sophia's voice roaring through the house.

"Diana, come get your son out of here! Let an old body rot in peace! The devil broke another glass!"

Diana smiles and shakes her head. She's obviously used to Carlo's clumsiness and Sophia's outbursts.

"That woman would drive a saint to drink," she mumbles under her breath as she leads me down a long hallway to the closet, where she grabs a dustpan and broom, then into the den.

Sophia rests on the couch, resembling a china doll herself with her body sprawled out on the cushions. Carlo sits beside her on the floor, looking angelic. Slivers of broken glass are scattered in the corner of the room and a puddle of water slowly seeps its way across the beautiful tongue-in-groove wood flooring. This room looks normal. There are no dolls here. Then I notice something that may possibly be even worse. A bear head, real, sticking out from the far corner of the wall. His teeth are big and white, curved menacingly at me. With a shudder, I turn away. This place is so strange. I don't like it here at all.

"Carlo! You apologize to Sophia right now. I've told you not to run in the house!"

"Sorry," Carlo says, lightly grabbing the old woman's hand. Sophia lets him clasp it for a moment before pushing him back. She looks at me, then fumbles with the collar of her robe. I can see the outline of her thin legs underneath her cotton blanket.

Carlo moves back from the couch. "Sorry, old lady," he mumbles under his breath.

Diana shoots him a harsh look. But Sophia doesn't seem to hear. She's too focused on me.

"Oh, hello, miss," she says. "Are you from the castle? Have you come to bring me back there?"

I look to Diana for help. But she's busy cleaning up the mess, shooing Carlo from the room, making sure all of the glass shards are gone.

"I'm Claire," I say, holding my hand out to Sophia, who clearly doesn't remember much.

"Nice to meet you, Claire. Thank you for coming to my house."

"You're welcome," I say, matching Sophia's formal tone.

She gestures me closer and I go, holding my elbows in close to my body as though to protect myself in some way that I can't quite fathom. Sophia is painfully thin, and I can't miss how her skin hangs on her face and on her arms. The smell of mothballs, old perfume, and medicine wafts up at me when she moves. I shrink back into myself, even as Sophia takes my hand. Her papery skin is old and crumbling, reminding me of illness and death, two things I've always been afraid of. When I was young, I used to wake in the middle of the night and stand in my parents' doorway, listening to the sound of their breathing, as if to reassure myself that they had made it through another night. Although I never told anyone that I was afraid if I didn't stand watch, they might pass away in the empty space between night and morning.

I'm sometimes filled with the same sliver of fear about losing Jim, too. When he sleeps, I lightly touch my hand to his chest, feeling the thump of his heart beating against my palm for comfort. Since I became pregnant, though, I had stopped being afraid and had begun to relax. With Lily's new form filling me up inside, I was suddenly filled with thoughts of life, instead of death. How ironic that her life slipped away when I wasn't even looking.

"Can I get you some gum?" Sophia asks now, jolting me back to the present. With gnarled fingers, she reaches for a pale pink Kleenex box on the table beside the couch, then rests the box of crumpled tissues on her lap. She rummages through them, dropping some on the floor as she moves, but she doesn't seem to notice.

"Aha! Here it is!" She whips out a mangled pack of Spearmint gum. "Have a piece." She hands me a slippery foil-wrapped stick, which seems worse for wear. The edges of the wrapper are torn and the gum looks old and stale. "Go ahead, try it," she insists.

I look to Diana again, but she's already left the room. Reluctantly, I unwrap the gum and pop the battered stick into my mouth. It tastes strongly of old peppermint and is so stiff it hurts my jaw to chew, but I'm afraid of upsetting Sophia or, worse yet, incurring her wrath.

"Now, who are you again? How did you get here?" Sophia asks, her hands pleating and unpleating the blanket. She looks at me blankly, as though I have just arrived.

"I'm Claire. Remember?"

"Claire *who*?" Sophia demands. "Who are you and what do you want?" Then she notices the gum wrapper I hold between my fingers. "Stop! Thief! Help, police! This woman stole my gum! HEEEEEEEEEELP!"

I cower back from Sophia, ducking my head away from her accusing glare. She's hit a nerve so deep inside me I didn't even know it was there. I *am* a thief, but not of her gum. I feel like I may have stolen Lily's life by being too complacent. I had so proudly stepped into the role of being a mother, shedding off my deepest fears as though I no longer needed them. In school, when I studied Mythology, the Greek gods always waited for someone like me to make one mistake so they could punish them for their carelessness. I should've known life would work like that, taking away the thing you cherish the most, teaching mortals not to value anything too much.

"I'm sorry," I say helplessly to Sophia, as though by getting her forgiveness I can also make the other thing right, the thing that I ache from. The pain stretches me deep inside the way Lily had stretched me, pulling my body to the point of breaking.

Diana comes running into the room and smiles apologetically at me as she tries to calm Sophia down.

"Hush, now, hush," she says, stroking Sophia's arm, her cheek, her leg, trying to soothe the old woman with the steadiness of her touch.

I chew the gum hard, seeking strength in the motion, finding my balance again as I watch the two women struggle.

"Get away from me!" Sophia screams, pushing at Diana with her crooked fingers, trying to knock the young woman down. The two woman wrestle for a bit, then Sophia seems to lose her venom and settles back down limply against the coach pillows, looking like a doll again instead of a wild animal.

As soon as I can, I escape from this horrible place. The cold air outside offers relief after the overpowering feel of the house. Yet particles of its smell linger in my hair, my coat, my skin. When I'm a safe distance away, I spit out the chewed gum into my palm, then slip the sticky wad back into the wrapper. Inside the silver foil, I roll it into a hard ball and throw it away in the tangled layers of grass on my way home to the lighthouse. But even hours later, the muscles in my jaw still ache.

Chapter 7

When I was young, I used to believe in ghosts. I was afraid to go to bed at night because I thought a ghost was living in my bedroom. While our house was in no way as gloomy and ominous as Sophia's, it was an extremely old house and there was lots of room for my imagination to conjure up a ghost that hid inside the thick walls. My parents spent many late nights trying to comfort me and convince me that there was no such thing, but no matter what they said, I didn't believe them. I saw the ghost in the shadows of the room, pictured a gauzy skeleton shape made of a pile of bones similar to those I had seen on a field trip with my class to the Museum of Natural History. Days, even months, later the image stayed with me, looming in my room, evolved into something real that lurked in the corners and wanted to hurt me.

As I grew older, the memory of the skeleton slowly faded and my impressions of ghosts relaxed into an uneasy feeling I couldn't explain. When I thought about it, I could narrow the feeling into a tiny pinprick of light just off to the side of my vision, and my heart would beat right up into my chest, knocking hard against my ribs hard. I'd always expected my parents to come running out from their bed to see what had happened to me.

I smile now, remembering my fear as I stand outside on the little bridge that leads from the lighthouse to the beach and wish that I could somehow regain my childhood faith and innocence again. It's so cold out—a frosty thirty-two degrees, the weatherman said on the radio this morning—that my breath comes out in tiny white puffs. They linger in the air and make me think of the way that childhood ghosts looked back then. Sometimes I thought I could hear that ghost creeping across my floor, causing the boards to creak. The sound thrilled and scared me at the same time.

In some ways I was petrified of the idea, and in other ways I also felt oddly privileged to have such a creature haunting me. It made me feel strangely special. Sometimes I liked to pretend the skeleton was a lady ghost who used to live in my room and had lost her child at sea in a shipwreck. She was haunting my room, hoping to find a way to meet up with the child. I imagined she wanted to wake me up and see if I would help her find him.

My parents' house creaked a lot, especially in the winter when the heat was on, so it wasn't hard in the dark to turn the noise into something more. And I don't think I made this idea up, really. I used to read a lot of books when I was young—supernatural mysteries and Nancy Drew and the Hardy Boys—and I must have gotten the story line from one of them. Over time, I was able to weave those details into my own scenario.

Now, as I watch the white mist of my breath shimmer and then slowly fade away until it dissipates, I think about Lily and wonder if she's a ghost-like cloud herself now. I like to think of her as something delicate, not like the creepy skeleton I had envisioned as a child. Maybe a white, gentle Lily blows in the air around me, dancing here in the wind, and I don't even know it. As silly as I know this is, and as much as I have outgrown the idea of ghosts, reconsidering the possibility gives me some comfort. I can imagine that other parents feel the same way when they lose a child, searching for some kind of hope or vision to hang on to, no matter if it's impractical or insubstantial. That's why some of them call in psychics to find missing children, and why many professional, logical people visit witchcraft stores, read their horoscopes regularly, and reach out for any other mental 'life rafts' in times of distress to keep them afloat.

I lean my elbows on the wooden railing of the bridge to think about this more. The sky here feels lower than it does on the mainland, almost as though I could just reach up and touch it. There are layers of different shades of blue that stack up in pieces, and when I squint my eyes I feel like I can split them apart with my vision. Maybe Lily is caught up there in the layers of air, trying to come down to be with me. But maybe she is stuck somewhere and can't seem to work her way free.

Even though this is a ridiculous thought, I feel my heart beat faster and my breath catch with the birth of the idea. Maybe my poor little Lily feels all alone and needs someone to comfort her. While I have my family and friends to help me if I need them, who is with my poor little baby to take care of her? She's probably just as upset at being separated from me as I am from her.

I've never thought about that before, but once the thought pops into my mind, it lodges there, and no matter how hard I try, I can't seem to rid myself of this uneasy feeling.

I go back inside and decide to take a bath to try to relax. I brought my favorite rose bath salts with me and I sprinkle them under running water in the tiny ceramic tub that's propped up on thick, clawed feet. The steady whirl of the generator that powers the lighthouse fills the cramped bathroom space and when I sink into the tub, the whole room vibrates slightly.

I lean back in the bath and close my eyes, eager to forget things. Even though the water is steamy and turns my skin pink, the air in the room is cold and I try to fit more of my body under the water. It isn't easy to get all of myself into such a small tub.

Imagine if Lily was here with me and I had to fit both of us in here together. I love looking at pictures of mothers and children taking baths together. There's something so sweet and innocent in the concept. I like the idea of fathers bathing their babies, too. I can envision what Jim would look like leaning over the tub, awkwardly holding a slippery Lily just underneath her arms, dunking her body carefully into the water the way he dunks part of his cookie into his coffee at night, careful not to let the whole thing fall in.

I start to drift off on these thoughts, which whirl around me in the steamy air. There's no fan, so soon the room turns heavy with condensation. I lean into the feeling and let my vision grow hazy. I had forgotten to turn on the light because the sun had still been streaming through the window. Now, as daylight fades, the room melts into a layer of darkness. I can make out the outline of shapes but no real forms. I know the sink is over there and the toilet in the corner, but it's hard to tell where one thing ends and another starts. Yet there's something comforting about all this obscurity.

Suddenly, a flash of light fills the room, catching me off guard. Could it be lightening? I jump up, splashing water onto the tile floor. My heart knocks hard against my chest and I can't quite catch my breath. It must be lightning, I tell myself, craning my head from the tub toward the window, hoping to see signs of a brewing storm. Although it seems too cold for rain, I know that the warmth of the ocean air prevents the island from seeing much snow at this time of year.

Just as suddenly as it appeared, the light fades away. But I feel my body stay tense and tight; the hairs on the back of my neck literally prickle. There's a strange stillness in the air, as if there were someone else in the room, followed by the slight sound of the door creaking. Or maybe it's the generator groaning. It's hard to tell from down here in the tub. Or maybe someone is there. "Lily?" I call. "Lily, is that you, my precious little baby?"

Chapter 8

In the light of day, I can't stop thinking about Lily. Her face is hanging in my mind, bigger than it was in life. Even in my sleep last night, she came to me and reached inside, pulling me out of the depths of my unconsciousness, wanting me to focus on her, not on the things that dreams are made of. She demanded that I give her all my attention. Now, in the morning, I feel like she's everywhere, has been everywhere, since the first moment the nurse had placed her in my arms five weeks ago. She hasn't really left me.

The first time I held Lily was a few minutes after her birth. I lay on the delivery table, still catching my breath and trying to come back from the dark place I had briefly crossed over into during the worst part of the labor. The nurse roughly jerked me back to earth by handing me this tiny red infant. For a second I didn't even realize it was my baby. But then I noticed how warm she was as she lay in my arms, barely squirming, making loud mewing sounds like a cat, and I could smell the most private part of myself lingering on her. I balanced her in my cupped palms, resting her miniature arm against the soft blue cotton of my hospital gown, afraid she would break if I moved too suddenly. Her skin felt softer than anything I'd ever touched. I couldn't stop stroking the side of my thumb over and over the thin, silky, wrinkled layer.

She was even smaller than some of the dolls I played with as a child, and it was hard to believe she was real and breathing. Yet I could see her tiny chest slowly moving up and down as she screwed up her mouth and sucked for air, as she got used to this new concept of breathing. I was still aching unbearably from the pain I had just endured, and yet holding Lily seemed to make it lessen, as if the pain was nothing compared to this beautiful human being who was here. She was really here, finally. And this realization was like taking the strongest pain killer there is, because even though I knew that the pain was still there and would probably remain for a while, it had moved away from my body and gone off to a corner, politely waiting while I got used to my daughter before it returned to attack me again in full force.

The baby snuggled against me, a tiny pink cap tugged over her head to keep the warmth in, and I stared down in fascination at her rosebud mouth and the crescent shape of her eyes and the thin legs dangling from her small form, hanging down almost as if they were boneless.

Then I remembered Jim, who had stepped out of the room briefly to call my parents. I wanted him here, wanted him to come and share this moment. He walked back in and smiled at me, watching from the doorway as I shifted Lily to make her more comfortable. Already I was becoming a pro at this mother stuff. It just took a little getting used to, but it seems to be true that there's some instinct in women that tells them what to do and how to do it. I patted the edge of the bed so Jim would join us and he came, a little shyly, as though he were in awe that I had delivered a real, live baby and this act had transformed me into someone else, someone new, someone he had to get used to again.

For both of us, it seemed like such a miracle to have a baby, even though of course people do it every day. But we just couldn't believe it had happened to us; although we had been planning for this moment for months and months, we had never quite understood it would feel as wonderful and right as this did.

We had not picked a name for the baby yet. We didn't decide on the name Lily until after she was gone. We had agreed several months before that we should wait until we saw our daughter to figure out what name would best suit her and in the first few minutes of getting to know her, we thought it was too soon to determine the name she would answer to for the rest of her life. (Later, after she died, she reminded us of the Easter lilies my parents had in a vase in their hallway each spring.)

"She's beautiful," Jim said soberly to me. "I can't believe she's really ours. This is so incredible." He struggled to find the right words, beaming like a child who's just been invited into his favorite store to pick out all the toys he wants and he's so thrilled he doesn't even know where to start.

"I know," I said. "I feel like this is all a dream and I'm going to wake up from it and she'll be gone. Can you imagine, this is our daughter!"

The baby, who had been sleeping in my arms, suddenly shifted as if she knew we were talking about her and her eyes scrunched up even tighter; then suddenly, brightly, they flickered open. She looked surprisingly sharp and clear for a baby, watching me watching her. I stared into their blue depths (she looked surprisingly sharp and clear for a baby, watching me watching her) and I marveled over how great, how healthy, how wonderful she was. She was such a pretty thing with all of her perfect toes and all her fingers and such little ears and a tiny snub of a nose. She was perfection if I've ever seen it.

Jim reached out and touched her tiny fist with his big, awkward hand, and Lily surprised us both by uncurling her fingers and taking Jim's thumb in her grip, squeezing hard. She had some real strength to her.

I think this was Jim's proudest moment thus far, standing there being clung to by his daughter. His usually serious face was transformed into something lighter and more carefree and his smile grew deeper and lacked the tension that usually kept it from spreading all the way up to his eyes. I have never seen him look so happy. I, too, was happier than I had ever been before, watching this big beautiful strong man go all soft at the touch of our brand-new baby. This made all the pain of childbirth completely worth it.

I would like to have had a photograph of that moment, capturing the way we looked: the three of us huddling together on the bed that way, tasting the newness of being a real family.

Here in the lighthouse, I often replay that scene in my mind, exploring the different textures and nuances. What was I feeling and thinking then? I try to recall each precious piece of the eight short hours that Lily lived. I've noticed that life is funny that way: when things go well, it's so easy to live in the moment and just sleepwalk blindly through the days without even registering the beauty and color and grace that surrounds us. But when things don't work out the way we had planned, we put our minds in reverse and try to see all the details and parts that we may have missed the first time around, living more fully in our remembrances than we ever did in real life.

Does Jim do this, too? I wonder, but have never thought to ask him. I don't know if this is a female thing or if the feeling surpasses gender differences and is universal. And even if Jim does do this, I'm forced to ask myself: to what end? Does it even count if he can't process these moments? I know Jim is sad about Lily's death, yet he somehow tries to act as if his grief doesn't touch him deep inside the way that mine does.

The morning sun pours into the lighthouse in full strength, easing, but not erasing, my worries about Jim, which haunt me quite often. To be fair, I know he's also very worried about me and the way I'm coping, or not, with everything. We're just so different. But I feel like things are getting easier for me now that I'm away and have a chance to put things into perspective. I wish he could have the same chance to find his way and accept what has happened. While part of Jim can be so sensitive and sweet, there's that other part of him that insists on being so unemotional. Sometimes I worry he won't be able to survive the harshness of the world because this second part keeps him from truly facing difficult things. Instead, he acts like they'll go away if he simply ignores them. I believe Jim has found a way to bury his feelings, but eventually they're bound to find their way back to the surface when he least expects it.

Jim often handles emotion by throwing himself into a project or physical activity and trying to drown himself in it so as not to think. For instance, since Lily died he's been working fourteen-hour days at the law firm and getting up at five every morning to go for a three-mile run. I, on the other hand, feel so overwhelmed by everything that I've just been moving in slow motion. He wants me to focus all of my energy on my own artwork and, in fact, right after Lily died he tried to get me to sign up for an art class. In the state I was in, this idea didn't interest me. I actually was angry at him for being insensitive enough to have even suggested it. He seemed completely baffled by my reaction, since we handle things so differently.

"I thought you'd *want* to take a class to take your mind off this," Jim said, running his fingers through his hair as he studied me, shaking his head, trying to figure out what in the world he could do to take away my pain.

The night before he had brought home my favorite ice cream, and that had set me off in tears. Chocolate chip cookie dough was what I ate when I had been pregnant with Lily.

Now here he was with a course book in his hand from the Boston Center for Adult Education. He had circled a seminar on advanced painting that he thought I would like. And once again I was crying and angry with him. He just couldn't win.

I knew, even as I threw the book across the room and stormed into the bedroom, that I should have appreciated his gesture. Jim was trying to help me in the only way that he was able to. And I knew he would do almost anything for me, save the *one* thing that I needed: I needed him to cry with me, and that was something he couldn't do.

Why couldn't Jim cry with me? I ask myself this for the umpteenth time as I sit in Ida's living room, my chair angled so I can see out the window without straining. The winter beach stretches out like a billboard flaunting a tropical paradise. The water is so blue, the sky so clear, the sand so pale from inside here. Everything looks so smooth and peaceful, even though I know it's actually starting to grow colder on the island as the season lengthens. Earlier in the day, my hands had gone completely numb through my gloves when I took a walk. I wonder if it's as cold back in Boston.

If Jim were to look out the window now from his office in Copley Square, he'd have such a different view. He'd see the trampled grass turning brown and old, people hurrying by, bundled up against the chill. Traffic jams on the street beneath his office, cars impatient to get through this busy section of the city. Everyone in a rush, no one taking the time to look around and enjoy his or her life. I feel sorry for Jim to be stuck in that madhouse. Poor Jim.

I decide to write to him and see how he's doing. I rip a piece of white paper out of my notepad and think for a moment, trying to get my thoughts in order before I begin.

Dear Jim,

Well, here I am in the lighthouse, getting back on my feet slowly but surely. I'm sorry it has taken me a while to respond to your letter. At first I was so overwhelmed by everything I couldn't seem to find the strength to even pick up a pen, let alone try to write to you. But you have been in my thoughts constantly, as I hope you realize. When I think of you suffering there in Boston in our apartment where we would eagerly have welcomed little Lily, my heart breaks and I feel as if I can hardly stand it. But here in this lighthouse, there are no memories of Lily. There is no nursery where she would have slept, no pile of stuffed animals we so enthusiastically collected over the past year. There is nothing here but peace and solitude. Nonetheless, it is here in this peace that I have found the will to reach out to our dear baby. I feel closer to her here than ever before. Even though I know Lily is forever gone, I hope that you, too, will find some way to embrace her memory.

Love, Claire

I seal the envelope and decide to walk down to the Main Street post office. I bundle up with extra layers of clothing and my warm coat then slip on my gloves and set out for some needed exercise.

There are two letters in my PO box from Jim, postmarked one day apart. There's also a letter from my mom, and one from the school where I work. I bring them all back to the lighthouse with me and snuggle down on the couch in the living room to read them.

The first letter from Jim is in his neat handwriting on our wedding stationery again:

James and Claire Edwards

Claire:

How're things? I guess I'm OK, other than a bad cold that won't seem to go away. Your mom was nice enough to bring me a big container of her chicken soup and I am hoping that will cure me soon enough. I've been having trouble sleeping at night and keep thinking of you and the day that we met. It was so long ago and I haven't thought about it in ages, but now all of a sudden the scene keeps playing in my head, larger than life. It is like we are two characters in our own movie. I can see the way that your blond hair looked in the sunlight and the brilliant way your green eyes sparkled. That little orange two-piece bathing suit looked so cute on you, too. I wonder if Lily would have grown up to look like you. I imagine she would have, huh? Funny that we met near the very lighthouse you are living at. If only we had known back then how things were going to play out. I had no idea all those years ago that someday we would actually be married. Anyway, I don't know why I am rambling on like this. Must be the Nyquil talking. I am getting tired of being in our bed alone and am asking you again—Please come home, where you belong.

Jim

Wow. While of course I've replayed that day in my mind so often while I've been here at the lighthouse, I'm surprised to have Jim remark on it. I'm still marveling at his letter—and the unexpected sentimental tone—as I lean back on the soft cushions of Ida's couch and open his second note. This is on yellow-lined legal paper. He probably scribbled it between clients at work, since his writing is sloppy and hard to read, with the letters running into each other. This is unusual for him; he's usually anal about being neat. My forehead puckers and my shoulders tense, as I hunch over by the lamp and try to make out his words.

Claire, Cold is still bad. When are you coming home? We got a delivery yesterday that caught me off guard. Remember the baby swing that was back-ordered last summer? It's here now, in our living room. I'd forgotten all about it. Should I return it, or put it in storage? J

I remember that swing. We had found it in a boutique in Maine last August when we were spending a weekend there for Jim's college roommate's wedding. The seat hangs down on a thick white chain that's suspended from a white metal frame. It has green vines and delicate pink roses painted like streamers twirling around the poles. The swing itself has a pink velvet seat and can be used upright to hold the baby sitting or can recline back like a little cradle to rock the baby to sleep. There was only a display model in the store, but the owner had promised to order a new one and have it sent to us as soon as it arrived. Funny how you forget about things like that.

For a second, picturing the swing causes my nose to sting with tears and I move my arm up to hold them back. My eyes feel a bit wet but I don't cry.

I have regained my composure and am completely dry-eyed when I open my mom's letter. Hers is on plain white memo paper.

Claire, dear:

I do not want to worry you at all, but Jim is not doing well. He has a bad cold and cough that I fear is turning into bronchitis, or worse, maybe even pneumonia. Maybe you could just come home for the weekend to take care of him and then go back to that place, that lighthouse, where you are living now. I have been running back and forth between your apartment and our house, which is wearing me down and I am afraid I cannot keep up this pace for much longer.

At mass on Sunday, Father Fogherty said a special prayer for Lily that I think you would have liked. I wish you had been there. Maybe he will repeat it this weekend if you come with me to church.

Love, Mom

The envelope from the school where I work is typed with my name and my island post office address. The letter folded inside is also typed, on official school letterhead.

Sudbury Elementary School
35 Townsend Turnpike
Sudbury, MA 02156
(508) 333-2500

November 10

Dear Mrs. Edwards:

I am the substitute art teacher filling in for you this year while you take your leave. This is my very first teaching job and I am enjoying the students and the experience immensely. I graduated from the Massachusetts College of Art in May and I have heard in the teachers' lounge from others that you also got your training there. It is nice to know we have our schooling in common. The Principal gave me your lesson plans for the year and I was wondering if you feel it important that I stick to them strictly. For my student teaching last year I had come up with some projects that I administered to the students and I was hoping you wouldn't mind if I incorporated a few of them into this year's plan. (Please understand that I don't want to ruin your approach and will respect your decision if you say no. But I thought it worth asking, anyway.) About your baby, I hear that something awful went wrong and she died. Please know that even though we never met, I am very, very sorry.

Yours truly, Sandy Gresson

I haven't even thought about school, or my students, until I read Sandy's letter. She sounds like a nice girl and I quickly write her a note back telling her to take as much liberty as she wants with the lesson plans. I don't mind a little creativity and I'm sure the kids will enjoy her excitement and enthusiasm for the job.

Jim's letters I answer next, telling him to take care of himself and see the doctor if he's not feeling any better soon. I decide not to write back to my mother yet. I know she wants me to go home to Jim and perhaps she's right. After all, he is my husband and I should be there to take care of him if he needs me, but I'm certainly not ready to leave yet.

Especially since I'm starting to think that Lily may somehow be here with me.

Chapter 9

I'm not very religious these days, and I don't accept the notion of God in a traditional way. Yet I do like to think there's some kind of plan for everyone in this world. I find a level of comfort built into the idea that our lives are all governed by some type of purpose and order. I guess that could be called 'Fate.' Like my meeting Jim. That, I think, was definitely supposed to happen. But my mother thinks this was much more than fate. She says that it's God who brought us together. She thinks I confuse the concepts of fate and faith, but I somehow believe they're interchangeable. My mother has tried for the past few years to convince me to believe in God and put myself in his hands. Or throw myself, is more like it, I suppose. She thinks that he could 'save' me. I don't think I need any saving, though, and most of the time I'm happy with myself the way I am. While this is a difficult time I'm grappling with, the truth is that until now, my life has gone pretty smoothly.

I know for some people religion is literally a 'God-send' and enables them to get through the day, but I don't think everyone needs to rely on it as much as my mother does. She's always trying to convert me to become a 'good Christian.'

She was raised as a Catholic and although she disagreed with some of the teaching of the Church back then, she turned to some of the more conservative ideals and tried to instill them in me when I was young. As I got older, though, she gave up. Over time, we deviated away from even going through the motions of practicing any formal religion. But then, a few years ago, she had an experience that changed everything. Her parents were killed in a car accident and suddenly she turned whole-heartedly to the church the way I imagine teenagers would turn to a cult in a time of uncertainty. My father, on the other hand, doesn't practice any faith. My mother often blames his lack of direction for ultimately corrupting me.

I don't mind if my mother wants to go to church every single morning as long as she doesn't impose this on me. But since Lily died she's been trying to get me to go along with her. She thinks in her strange way that if I'd gone to church and prayed and believed in God, he never would've taken away my baby. She would never, ever voice this thought aloud, but, nonetheless, I know that she's thinking it.

I forgive her for this harshness because I know it's what she also thought about herself when her parents were killed. She blamed herself for letting it happen. If she'd been more religious, she reasons, God would have been watching her and would have prevented their deaths.

I understand that by blaming the tragedy on herself, my mother was able to find a way to feel in control of the situation. But her current beliefs also give her a false sense of power. Since she does go to church frequently these days, she thinks she's in good standing with God. She revels in the idea that this allows her to keep the rest of us safe. She couldn't keep Lily safe, though, so she needs to blame me. That's how her mind works.

I know that Jim doesn't 'blame' me at all for Lily's being born with a heart defect. He's a reformed Jew and in his way of thinking, the concept of blame feels somewhat different. He knows that prayers couldn't have saved Lily. On the same day that she was born, her little heart just stopped. Nothing we, or the doctors, could have done would have prevented it. Jim says this was just the way things were meant to be. I like his perspective much better than my mother's.

I also like the fact that the Jewish faith, from what I gather, doesn't focus on guilt in the same way that my mother does. When Jim talks about guilt, it's usually in the context of something he forgot to do, like sending a birthday card to his aunt, who turned 83 last month. I've heard the phrase "Jewish guilt," but for Jim that concept just doesn't exist.

There's a bad part to Jim's beliefs, too. He thinks that when someone dies, that's just the end of it. Jim doesn't believe in heaven or angels or afterlife. He thinks that Lily is—to put it bluntly—just dead.

I think my beliefs fall somewhere between Jim's and my mother's. I like a lot of the concepts of Judaism, but I find it impossible to believe that the tiny plot of dirt in the cemetery, which doesn't even have a headstone yet to mark it, is really where my baby lies.

At the funeral, even through my tears for what would never be, I reached deep into my soul to grasp onto the knowledge of the afterlife, and the hope that Lily had moved on to somewhere better. I have no picture in my mind of what heaven will look like, but the very concept fills me with a sense of relief and peace that's so deep and rich it flows through my veins like nothing else I've ever experienced.

The cemetery was cold and I huddled against Jim, tightly gripping his arm with my nails, pulling on his jacket so hard in my grief that I thought I would rip it. Jim cupped me to him, letting me lean into his warmth, as though he were trying to transfer some of his strength to me. I could feel a ribbon of heat flowing through the layers of his clothes and making them wet. It made me wonder if he does cry, but his tears come out in the form of sweat rather than streaming down his face, like mine do. My tears came out in heavy gushes of salty water that burned my skin and made my eyes ache.

My father and my uncle were the pallbearers, a blur of dark jackets and hair carrying the red-velvet-lined casket, the smallest one I have ever seen. They were bringing it over to the freshly dug hole in the ground. Was Jim wishing his parents were alive to be here with him? I had all my family around and I felt sad that he had no one here except for me. His elderly aunt, who had helped to raise him, was in ill health and couldn't make the plane ride from Michigan. And there was no one else in Jim's family still alive. But this fact didn't seem to faze him.

I found myself studying the richness of the turned-over earth, which was darker than I would have expected. I wondered if it was difficult to dig in the ground when the weather was this cold. Pieces of dirt clung to the edges of the grave, as though they didn't want to be completely displaced.

The priest from my mother's church stood only a few feet away from me, and the crisp air raised his voice up as if it were a loudspeaker. But even as I heard his words clearly, I found it hard to focus on them. There seemed to be some kind of disconnect from my ears to my brain that refused to give meaning to the weight of the sounds and the syllables. There was something about ashes and dust, and turning back to the earth, and the loss to the parents of the new baby, Lily. I watched everything from such a distance that it all blended together and I found my mind wandering away to other times and other places.

I thought of the beach where Jim and I met, and the grateful way he sometimes looks at me when he thinks I'm still asleep, and how my mother always told me not to walk alone at night in the park because something horrible could happen to me. She didn't realize that danger could be lurking right in my own house.

Then Jim refused to let me float off in my mind to escape the reality of the funeral. He pulled me back to the cemetery with the weight of his hand on my back.

"It's time," he whispered, and I looked at him, and at my surroundings, blankly. Time for what? I wondered. This day was all such a confusing mixture of pain and hurt and things I didn't want to face.

Jim looked white, tired, and shaky as he handed me the long white lilies we had bought that morning on the way to the funeral. He helped me to the casket and we gently arranged the flowers on top of the tiny gilt-edged case. We had chosen the most expensive casket they made. After all, we knew it was the one and only thing we could ever give to Lily.

The lilies were longer than the casket's length and I thought there must be some irony in that, only I couldn't think of what it was. I couldn't think of what anything was anymore. I even forgot to let go of the flower stems as the casket began to move into the yawning hole, and Jim had to gently pull me back, prying my fingers from their clench on the green stems.

That awful, yawning hole, that's all I could see, and I pulled out of Jim's grasp, wanting, and yet not, to watch as the casket was lowered.

There in its grave the casket finally rested, several feet below the surface, too far away from me. I had that panicked feeling that reminded me of the time I had been washing dishes and my wedding ring had slipped off my finger and been sucked down the drain. I was frantic to get it back but found my hands wouldn't fit into the tiny opening to retrieve it. (Later, a plumber had gotten it back.) Again, I was filled with the same kind of pain. Only now I knew that was Lily in there, my baby, not a ring, and I couldn't reach her, though I tried. And no plumber could help this time. Perched on my high heels, I bent my knees and leaned forward, teetering there, wanting to see how far down it was to the bottom. Where was Lily hiding down there?

I buried my face in my hands. I don't know for how long. The next time I looked, the hole was gone. There was just a mound of moist dirt in its place and I wasn't sure whether this was good or bad. I just knew I could no longer see my baby. The dirt was a dark patch against the drying winter grass. I guess then the funeral was over because people were moving away, heading for the row of cars off by the street somewhere. For a moment, I found I was too weak to walk, and my legs gave way beneath me. But then Jim was there to hold me up and I was filled with a rush of gratitude for this man, my husband, who stood by my side and supported me, and that knowledge helped my head clear and grow sharper again.

I remembered I was here at the cemetery because my baby had died, and we had come here and buried her. Now we were done. Then I remembered something else, too. Something that I had known at one time but then forgotten: I remembered that the casket contained Lily's frail white body only—not her soul. This knowledge filled me with a soothing river of calm flowing throughout my tense and weary body.

Standing there in front of the tiny plot of land, I felt transported back to the hospital room, to the moment when Lily took her last breath. I knew she had been lifted up out of her skin and had floated above me. In my bed across the room from where the doctors worked on Lily, I had *felt* the very second when she stopped being one of us and became a part of the universe. I could see her formless presence hovering in the air, making the light quiver with her force, and I had smiled and reached out to her with my eyes even as I felt my stomach twist into a deep pain, knowing that I'd never hold her again.

Chapter 10

When I found out I was pregnant with a girl, I went out and bought a beautiful baby dress. It was the palest pink fabric and had white smocking on the chest with little red flowers appliquéd on it and a rounded white collar. I found it in the baby department in Lord & Taylor and the price was astronomical—eighty-five dollars, which I found hard to justify—but I was excited at the prospect of having a little girl and decided to spring for it. Jim and I could certainly afford it, but with so many changes to plan for, we were trying to be practical.

I knew I was going to stop working soon and we wanted to save up for nursery school and start a college fund and turn Jim's study into the baby's room, all things that would cost lots of money. But along with the dress, I also had to buy white tights with a ruffle on the back, little white patent leather shoes, size zero, and a pink stretchy hair band with a bow to complete the outfit.

I marveled over the smallness of these baby things and the softness of the fabrics. I was afraid Jim would scold me when I came home, telling me I had spent too much on such frivolous items. But he's a sentimental man underneath his stoic front and when he held the dress in his hand, the chiseled lines of his jaw softened as though the weight of these purchases cemented something. They made our daughter real for him in a way that feeling the baby's kicks against my stomach at night with his palm hadn't quite done.

"I can't believe we're really gonna be parents," he said.

"I'm gonna be a dad!" His voice was thick with pride, and his eyes, which change with his mood, were brighter and more intense than usual.

Like me, he's an only child, so the dress, with all its elaborateness, was such a foreign thing to him. He ran his thumb over the tiny details as if he might be quizzed on them later. This was probably the first infant's clothing he had ever held. Seeing Jim awkwardly fingering the tiny outfit made me go soft inside and made my legs quiver.

I could imagine he was picturing a pretty little girl tightly clasping his hand as they walked down the street together. I know some men hope for their first child to be a boy, but I think Jim was secretly pleased that our baby was going to be a daughter. I was pleased, too, and could envision Jim spoiling the baby, who I hoped would look like him. She would give him someone besides me to belong to and I thought that was a good thing. Sometimes I worried that I, alone, wasn't enough of a family for Jim.

He would be such a great dad, too, I knew. I could tell in the tender way he touched me, nursing me through bouts of the flu, insecurities and fears, and the difficult parts of my pregnancy with the utmost patience.

But even though I've always been able to see the father in Jim, he had questioned whether he ever wanted kids. Yet I think his indecision stemmed from fear, not from a lack of desire. Jim didn't have to put these feelings into words, though. I could see them without his having to say anything. One of the nice things about our relationship is that I can often read Jim's deepest thoughts, conflicts, and desires, the way a deaf person reads lips, using his expressions to guide me through the maze of his denial.

Jim gently rested the baby's outfit on our bed and pulled me tight in his arms, as though I were a baby, too, his first baby, and he held me there for a while, silently rocking me to his chest.

"I love you, Claire," he whispered into my hair, the words so soft and blurred and beautiful.

I buried my nose in the wool of his sweater, breathing in the familiar scent as though I could save this memory for later.

"I love you, too," I whispered back. "I love you more than anything." I had waited so many years to hear Jim say those words, and for me to be able to say them back, even four years into our marriage, still seemed like a miracle.

Now, from Ida's bed in the lighthouse, I marvel over how much I really do love Jim. Even though we're far apart—a distance of slightly over a hundred miles separates us—I can see how he looks right now. I imagine him sprawled out in our bed, maybe sleepless, too, with his cold, and I can see the way his legs are tangled in our comforter, sky blue with thin white stripes, different from the one I sleep beneath here. I'd brought my old, down-filled bedspread with me when I came to the lighthouse, craving the familiarity of the soft, white background with a garden of tiny pink flower sprigs blooming in generous clusters.

This floral cover comes from the days before I married Jim. It's been sitting up on a shelf in the hall closet of our apartment for ages—I loved it too much to give away—and we only take it down when guests come and sleep on our pull-out couch in the study, which we had recently converted into Lily's nursery. I feel like a precious part of me is captured in the cotton duvet layer that holds the warm feathers close to give warmth and weight to the sleeper. Even though it's quite cold out now, though, the blanket feels too hot for the room and I struggle to push it off me, wishing I had Jim's weight against me instead.

I wonder if he could be thinking about Lily right now and

about that beautiful pink baby dress, and if he sees it in his dreams the way I do. Every few nights, in the rare moments when I do sleep, I see Lily in the dress but usually she looks much older and is standing on a street corner, somewhere I don't recognize, as if she's there waiting for me.

We buried Lily in that dress. She looked as beautiful as I had imagined she would when I bought it, though in my hopes she was wearing the dress as she squirmed on our living room rug, getting ready to explore our apartment. I had baby-proofed all our kitchen cabinets with special locks and put all the cleaning supplies away out of her reach, because friends with babies reminded me that the time goes so fast that before I would know it, Lily would be learning to crawl.

In reality, though, when the mortician put her in the dress—the one and only time anyone ever dressed her, he had to roll the sleeves up twice. The buttons were so tiny, too. There were four of them down the back, and I wonder now if his fingers trembled when he fastened them. He's used to death, though, so maybe it didn't upset him. But sometimes I imagine the way he might have looked, holding her little embalmed body in his large hands.

I had never touched anyone dead before, but when we got to the funeral home I leaned over and stroked Lily's cheek with the back of my hand.

It wasn't scary at all the way I'd imagined it would be. I felt more like Lily was asleep with her eyes closed. She'd soon wake up from a nap and be ready for a feeding. My full breasts tingled at the thought. Funny how the mind helps you cope with things too awful to imagine by reverting you back to playing that childhood game of Pretend.

Jim was standing off to the side, talking to my father,

and I don't know where my mother was. I was in a daze from the last few nights of not being able to sleep, so I stood there by myself and stared long and hard at Lily. She lay there frozen like a pretty little doll. I had an irrational urge to take her out of the box and play with her.

The room was beautiful, almost like someone's house, and I felt almost as if we were visiting a family friend or a relative instead of here to pay our last respects to Lily.

The funeral home was a big white building with strong pillars in front and a black door and shiny black shutters. It had a well-manicured lawn and well-clipped shrubs carefully framing the first floor. I had driven by many times over the years and once, as a child, I remember asking my mother who lived in the nice white house. She had explained to me what the building was. I was filled with curiosity then and wondered what the inside looked like.

Now here I was inside, which was as pretty as you'd expect, with the flat red carpeting and the smooth, vanilla-colored walls. The doors seemed very thick and heavy. Lily's casket was in a room on the first floor facing the road. I knew for the rest of my life, I would take detours through the town to avoid driving past here.

There were beautiful flowers everywhere, the pastel buds forming a lush garden and filling the room with the scent of a summer day. This peaceful image was at odds with the slow, heavy way I was feeling. I leaned over all the flowers to where the casket lay in the middle, and I cupped the back of Lily's head, lifting it a bit from the cushioning inside the wooden box. I could feel the soft down of her hair brush against my fingertips. The hair felt smooth and delicate, sort of like the thin line of hair that outlines Jim's shoulder blades and the back of his neck, but his hair has a rougher texture than Lily's soft fuzz.

The red roses on Lily's special dress matched the velvet

lining of the casket so perfectly you could almost think that I had planned it.

Here in the lighthouse, I still see Lily lying in that dress, see the way she looked at that moment. Even though five weeks have passed since then, it feels like minutes since when we buried her. I lie here in Ida's bed and try to escape the vision of Lily's form surrounded by flowers, but no matter which way I turn, she follows me.

The room is ripe with Lily's presence. Jim is here, too. Jim, Lily, and the pink dress. They are all surrounding me, these haunting visions. They have me caught in their grip, squeezing, squeezing me, refusing to let me sink into the welcome release of sleep.

But eventually I do work my way free and sink into an uneasy state of oblivion. This freedom is only temporary, though. Minutes, or maybe hours, pass, and then I wake again, feeling as though time is frozen in place, holding me captive with no hope anytime soon of seeing daybreak.

And then I'm forced to lie here, too tired to move or even to think anymore, and I listen to the sound of the waves crashing outside the lighthouse in steady beats that remind me of a funeral song. Ironically, that thought, even more than the memory of the dress and all the flowers, plunges me over the edge and draws warm tears across my cheeks even as I tell myself I will *not* cry. But I can't help seeing Lily in that little casket. Watching her in my mind, I see her chest move and then I start thinking that maybe, somehow, she *is* still alive.

Chapter 11

After a sleepless night, I decide to take an early morning walk on the beach. It's quite frosty out and the wind is blowing so hard it whips my hair into my face. I push the strands out of my eyes and as I do, I notice a white mist hanging in the air with a glowing shimmer of light from the lighthouse tower behind it. Curious, I move toward the spot. What in the world could that be?

As I get closer, the mist begins to take form and suddenly, with a jolt, I realize what it is—the ghost of a small child. *Oh, my God!*

My whole body trembles at the sight. It's such a beautiful child, a little girl, with soft blond hair and a long, white, flowing dress. For a quick moment, before I have time to process this, my maternal instincts kick in and all I think about is how much I want to reach out and hug her.

Lily? Could this be Lily?

I have played around with the idea that maybe, somehow, she's been here with me all along. But it's only now, standing here with the bulb from the lighthouse tower spraying the air with soft white flashes of light, and listening to the crunch of the waves rolling off the ocean, then being sucked back again, that I truly, truly believe this. My Lily is here.

You have to have lost someone to understand how I feel right now, but it's as if God—the God that my mother firmly believes in—is giving me a second chance. It's almost impossible to describe the elation coursing through me. A heavy black cloud lifts off me and time rolls back to remind me of how I used to feel in the days before Lily's death, when I was happy. It's as simple as that: I'm happy again.

I stand here on the beach, feeling the happiness flow through me, and I watch Lily. I have to admit my joy is tinged with a thin layer of fear, but it's easy to push any hesitations away and embrace this wonderful discovery. I'm lifted up by the knowledge I've found my baby again. She looks so delicate that I would imagine the wind could knock her over with one solid gust. But I quickly notice that this doesn't seem to be the case. Instead, she seems to float right along with the breeze, not fighting it, her feet skimming the ground so lightly I can hardly believe it.

But then, I can hardly believe any of this. Is this real or am I dreaming? I haven't slept well for so long I wonder if I could have passed out right here as I walked along and maybe none of this is really happening. So I blink my eyes, hard, a few times to see if that will wake me up. Half of me is hoping with the speed of the blinking motion the floating girl will be gone, and the other half of me desperately wants her to stay here so I can greet her. I'm aching to rest my hand against her china-white skin and smell her sweet baby fragrance once again.

The second half of me wins, for it seems I could blink a million times and she refuses to disappear. She hangs here, suspended inches above the frozen sand in the cold air, like a dancer caught at the end of a leap from which she can never land. She watches me, watches my every move. I can see her big blue eyes following me to see what I'll do next.

It has been more than twenty years since I thought there was a ghost living in my childhood bedroom, and back then, that ghost had no face or shape. That ghost, if that's indeed what it actually was, was more of a noise and a feeling keeping me up at night in the dark and making me scared to go to sleep. I used to fight against it, working to keep it outside of my vision. This ghost now, though, is something completely different. Something to grasp onto and keep. This ghost (Or could she be an angel? I like to think of Lily as an angel) is of my own flesh and blood. I know it deep down in my bones, the way other mothers say they just know things that defy all logic and reason. And, after all, I *am* a mother. Once again I have become Lily's mother. Beautiful Lily. How wonderful it is to see her again.

Even though this ghost—or angel—is a little girl, not a baby, I recognize the set of Lily's eyes, so like Jim's, and the shape of the face with the rounded cheeks and the chin that comes to an elfish point like mine does. This is the Lily that appears at night in my dreams. Only now it isn't night and I'm standing here upright, quite far from asleep. I pinch my hand to make sure and am satisfied when I see the red bite my nails leave on my skin. I shiver at the thought of what this all means, even as I take the idea and wrap my mind around it so tightly it can't escape me. I'm desperate to keep my baby here with me and I move toward her, wanting to make her stay safe with me in the lighthouse forever. I want never to let her get away from me again.

Lily stands there, motionless, watching me. Slowly I inch toward her, taking tiny steps so as not to startle her. And as I move, the little girl—she looks about three, I would guess—seems to grow smaller and younger before my eyes. I think each day in heaven must be like weeks or months on earth, so Lily has grown up quickly there, but now back on earth the years are slipping off her again.

As I get closer, I hear her call out to me.

"Mommy, oh, Mommy. I miss you so much. Please hold me, Mommy," she says, her voice a beautiful melody gently floating on the ocean air.

And then I reach Lily and stretch out my arms to take this ephemeral girl up into a hug and at the instant I touch her silky presence, she becomes the baby again Jim and I had buried. Only she's not buried in the ground anymore; she's back with me again. I hold the baby in my arms the way that I ached to hold Lily one last time right after she had died. She was so still and white then, in death, and although she still looks so translucent now, she's here with me and that's all that matters. Nothing more.

I stand here holding Lily and smiling at her and she smiles at me and I see again how well this name fits her. The waves lap against the shore like a lullaby, and my arms ache from cradling Lily tightly to me.

Then I begin to sing to Lily, my voice echoing in the frosty air and blending in with the roar of the seagulls overhead. I sing a foreign nursery rhyme my mother used to sing to me when I was a little girl, and I've been waiting for most of my adult life to sing this song to my own baby. In fact, a few months ago Jim and I practiced singing this together as we cuddled on our bed and we wondered, then, if the baby could hear us inside my womb.

Since Jim is usually more formal and not one to let himself step into a silliness of a children's song, the experience uncurled a ribbon of hope that with the baby's birth, we would both find a way to let down our guards and grow into our new roles as parents.

Now I watch Lily's body relax into the song and her pale eyelids close as she drifts off to sleep.

Finally, I decide it's time to take the baby inside so she doesn't catch a chill. Do ghosts get sick? I'm unsure of this but to be on the safe side, I hold her close against my warmth and imagine I can feel her tiny heartbeats even though I know this is impossible. My head swims and my eyes feel cloudy in the fog of the morning, but the lighthouse shines against the blue sky like a beacon calling me home and I bring Lily inside with me, wanting to keep us both safe here in this place where I now believe anything can happen. After all, she is my miracle, isn't she?

Later, I sit on the couch inside the lighthouse and watch Lily sleep before me. I feel quite like someone else, not like my '"Claire self" today. Lily is safely nestled inside a big basket Ida uses to store her magazines. Now the magazines lay piled on the floor and Lily sleeps against a flowered couch cushion lining the bottom of her makeshift cradle. I've covered her with a soft white blanket I took off the back of the couch. Her face almost matches the pale woolen fabric. I sit and stare at her perfect little face and at the way her tiny hands curl. She doesn't look even a second older now than when I saw her in the casket. I only wish Jim could see her, too. How proud he would be of our beautiful little girl. But somehow we have ended up doing our mourning alone, so he's not here to share this moment with me.

I think about this and feel so sad for Jim, and sad for myself, too, because living with Jim those few weeks after Lily died had been so lonely. I hate the way he's pulled away from me in this terrible time and tries to act like he doesn't need me. While I know Jim and realize this is how he handles difficult things, I couldn't stand to be living with the heat of this man so close and yet knowing deep inside I was really alone. I just couldn't bear it. That's really why I had to come here to get away. More and more I find myself realizing how much I still love Jim with every bit of my soul, yet I also hate the part of him that closes off when things become challenging, although I suppose in coming to the lighthouse, I have done the same thing. I shrug this insight away and instead focus on Lily.

Watching her, I feel a deep peace flow through me and I feel one layer of the pain I've been carrying around inside for so long begin to flow away the same way bath water runs down the drain in the tub. This sense of relief gives me the time to focus on another layer of pain, which is inherent in my relationship with Jim.

Although sometimes Jim can be quite sweet, at other times he's too focused on himself and on his own defenses that he blocks me out from his life and makes me feel very alone and scared. There are so many times, especially since Lily's death, that I've reached out my hand and tried to touch his arm, tried to connect with the warm, wonderful person hidden inside him, but his shell is too thick for me to penetrate and all I can feel is the fabric of his shirt and I can't seem to get past that to the heart of this man. Then I'm left all empty inside and hurt and my whole body shakes. Even though I haven't seen Jim for a few weeks, I remember this feeling so well it cuts right through me and makes me feel a little sick with the intensity of it.

I remember one time in particular—the morning Jim drove me home from the hospital after Lily's death.

This wasn't the ride home I had imagined we would have. I had thought I would be sitting next to Lily in her car seat and cooing to her and making silly faces to make her smile as she got her first taste of the car's motion. It would have been such a happy time, and Jim and I would have felt so warm and excited to bring the baby home and to greet the guests who would come to see her.

But instead, here we were, without the infant seat and without Lily. It was only the two of us now and we were so silent together. I sat upright against the leather back of the front seat and folded my hands tightly in my empty lap, trying to cover the fact something was missing.

Jim stared straight ahead as he drove, not even glancing

at me to see how I was doing. I felt miles away from him even though he was so close I could smell the mango shampoo he had used on his hair that morning and could see the fine hairs on the back of his hand as he gripped the steering wheel so hard his knuckles went white with the effort. Seeing those knuckles released some tension inside me that had been building up and suddenly I lost my composure and began to cry. My sobs sounded hoarse and ugly in the silence of the car.

I looked to Jim, waiting for him to turn to me and offer me comfort. I didn't want much, just for him to shift his eyes toward me for a moment. *Please, Jim, look at me*, I silently pleaded. I felt then that if he had touched me or even looked at me, I would have known things would somehow, eventually, be all right again.

But he wouldn't even glance over at all. This fact filled me with a gripping rush of loneliness stronger than anything I had ever felt before.

I could barely breathe when this realization hit me. I choked on my tears and turned away, staring blindly out the smudged car window, wishing Jim would disappear. I couldn't help but feel he had failed me. A touch or a look is such a little thing to need, but Jim is stingy with those things when he's feeling threatened by emotion. In the back of my mind, I knew the real reason Jim couldn't offer me this was that he had been afraid he would cry himself if he looked at me, but this didn't make me feel any better. In fact, it filled me with a deep, painful anger, twisting my stomach in knots and giving me a throbbing headache.

As soon as we got home, I went into the bedroom and lay down on top of the comforter. My body felt old and beaten down, not only from the trauma of childbirth but also from all the emotional upheaval that had come afterward. It was as if time had slowed and I had gone through years of pain since I had left here three days earlier. I was so tired and sad and so alone, and sleeping or being with people didn't help ease any of this.

Later Jim came into the room and lay down stiffly beside me, careful to keep his healthy body from brushing against my sore one. I was still crying inside, but I pretended to be asleep because I didn't want to have to deal with him. He lay there, listening to the even sound of my breathing before he leaned over and gently touched my hair, smoothing my bangs off of the sticky heat of my forehead. Then he kissed the tender spot there. I felt my eyes sting at his touch, but I willed my body to stay motionless. I refused to touch Jim back, because he had not cried yet. Until he did, I wouldn't reward him. I wanted to punish him for refusing to release his pain the same way I did. Tears seemed like such an obvious response to death. Why couldn't Jim grasp this simple concept?

I finally did fall asleep and in my dreams, an imaginary Jim was sobbing uncontrollably. But instead of filling me with peace, this image felt surprisingly disconcerting. When I woke several hours later, I leaned over Jim's sleeping form and studied his face in the moonlight, seeking signs of dried tears to confirm the fact my dream was real. But his skin appeared dry and pale. He had *not* cried. That, I was sure of.

With all these thoughts crowding my mind now in the lighthouse, I decide to write to Jim again. It's strange that I haven't heard from him in a few days. I wonder if his cold is better by now. I'm pretty sure it hasn't gotten any worse, because if he were sicker, I know my mother would have contacted me right away. Therefore, I think his silence must stem from something else. Something I don't want to examine too closely.

Dearest Jim:

I am feeling very strange but very, very happy today, and I would like to think this letter finds you in good spirits yourself. It's been getting colder by the day—the weatherman reported a nippy 28 degrees this morning—and my toes were numb when I took my morning walk. But a very wonderful thing happened as I strolled along the sand and thought about everything. I started to feel more at peace with Lily's death and I started to question life and death in a new way.

I even started to find some different answers than I have ever found before. I want to share my newfound knowledge with you. I think I can finally, finally, cope with Lily's death and I think I can help you accept the way things have happened, too, when I next see you. I also realize that I have left you alone in your grief and am not there to hold your hand when you wake in the middle of the night. (Do you ever wake in the middle of the night in a panic the way I do?) Our coping styles are so, so different that the real truth is I could not stand your brave face and calm demeanor for another second. Why couldn't you cry with me, Jim?

I don't sign the note. I simply fold it and place it in an envelope. Then I put on my coat. I'm ready to go to the post office and mail it right away. I feel so anxious to get these fragile thoughts I've captured into words right into Jim's hands. As I turn to lift Lily out of her little wicker basket and take her with me, I suddenly realize she's gone. *Oh no!* It's as if she has evaporated back into the very air that brought her to me. The basket sits there, forlorn without her in it. The cushion inside and the white blanket I had used to cover Lily are the only things present. I reach down and stroke the softness of the blanket's pale wool, the way I would stroke the fur of a dog or a cat, and I let the smoothness against my fingertips offer a welcome escape from the confusion of the moment. Then I move my hand to rub the scratchy wicker surface and measure the difference between the two textures. There's something about touch that makes me turn to it in times of emotion. When I was dating Jim, whenever I was very sad or very happy, I remember I would lean the palm of my hand against the coolness of a wall or a couch or a tabletop, needing to find some kind of an anchor.

Now, I find myself needing the same kind of anchor to help me deal with all the strange and difficult things I'm suddenly faced with. I can't bear the thought that I've lost Lily again.

But then with the weight of the basket under my hand, I find myself able to reach up and find some answers. I know that ghosts come and go at will, appearing when the living most need them. So maybe Lily has served her purpose for the day and won't be back until tomorrow. This idea makes me feel a little better and also serves to remind me of something else: I'm lucky to have Lily at all, even for random, unplanned moments. With this thought firmly in my mind, I bravely pull out the white blanket and fold it neatly in thirds, placing it back into the basket, ready for when Lily returns.

Chapter 12

Time in the lighthouse seems to pass very differently than time in the city. Sometimes an hour flies by in what feels like minutes. Other times, five minutes feels like an eternity and I stare hopelessly at the clock on the wall by the window, praying for it to hurry up and show three, then four, then five o'clock. I look forward to its being late enough to eat dinner. Mealtimes are a solid way to mark the various stages of the day. Lily doesn't need to eat, though. She's such a young thing that she usually sleeps, cuddled in my arms or snug in the basket.

In the mornings, I'm usually still sleepy from my restless night and need something simple to ease me into my life. For breakfast I make some hot cereal with cinnamon and sugar on top. The steam from the warm milk makes the granules crystallize. There's something comforting about the smooth liquid sliding down my throat and landing in my stomach, where it sits for the early part of the day and warms me. For lunch, I make a sandwich or eat the leftovers from dinner the night before. I don't have much appetite but refuse to let myself skip any meals. Although I'm relatively slim, I do usually have to watch what I eat in order to maintain my figure. But since Lily's death, I find I don't have to worry about my weight at all. The bulk I had put on during the pregnancy, about twenty-five pounds, seems to have disappeared miraculously. When I get out of the shower,

I can see the faint curve of my ribs again in the bathroom mirror.

Dinner is my favorite meal. I can pass an hour or two preparing it. I try to vary the menu each day, making pasta one night and a pot pie the next. Sometimes I make lasagna or meatloaf or a big crock of soup with a crusty loaf of bread. When I feel really lonely or sad, I finish the meal off with some type of chocolate treat. Brownies, cupcakes, and Hershey bars all serve to cheer me up a little. And a cup of hot chocolate in the evenings helps to relax me and makes me feel more ready to go to sleep.

Every few days I head to the local market to replenish my supply of food and find something different to add to the selection. I can't carry much at a time, and going more frequently gives me something to look forward to. Besides my few encounters with Diana and Sophia, talking to the cashier is the only contact I've had with anyone. The thing I like best is that no one at the store knows who I am or knows about Lily's birth, death, or reappearance. I relish the ability to be invisible here. No one looks at me with pity or whispers behind my back about the tragedy I suffered. I am nameless and blend in with the other islanders.

Some days Lily is here in the lighthouse with me. Other times, she's gone. There doesn't seem to be any rhyme or rhythm to her presence, but she floats in and out at will and I find myself always on edge, always waiting for her. I've heard similar stories from others who have suffered a loss and found the spirit of their loved one returning to them. Sometimes the dead person comes back in his or her original form; other times it's in the body of a cat or a dog, but the spouse or parent recognizes the spirit inside as belonging to the one he or she has lost.

One mother feels her deceased daughter's hand on her shoulder at night. A father sees his daughter's face hovering in the sky. Lots of stories like these are out there. Different people describe their experiences in different ways, but while the circumstances vary a lot, the feeling is the same. There's always a sense of relief and peace that fills the survivor after the visit.

Today, I'm waiting for Lily and wondering when, or if, she'll decide to appear to me. Sometimes I don't actually see her in the room, but I can tell she's nearby. I feel like she's hovering right out of sight, waiting for me to discover her.

This time when the feeling hits, I'm sitting on the edge of Ida's bed, trying to decide if I should take a nap. I've been reading a book about grief and the stages of mourning, but it's way too dry and technical and the words all blur into meaningless sentences that have nothing to do with me.

Restless, I put the book down and stretch, and then a strange rush goes through me and I can't seem to place the feeling. I get up and wander aimlessly around the little room, trying to figure out what it is I'm looking for. There's this urgent sense that Lily is here somewhere, and that maybe she's trying to guide me to her. This is sort of like the game of hide and seek I used to play with my friends when I was young.

Now, though, the game simply frustrates me. I get up and pace around the room, squinting in the glare of the afternoon sunlight that pours into the room. *Lily? Lily? Where are you?* I lift up the pillow and she's not there. She's not under the desk, either. Then I go into Ida's closet, which is filled with her winter clothes and shoes and boxes. I keep my own clothes in my suitcase since there's no possible room to cram anything else into the crowded space.

I see no Lily here, yet her absence doesn't discourage me. In fact, I feel like Lily is leading me to something. I find myself going farther into the small black cave, pawing my way through silky dresses and fuzzy jackets and the cold metal of belt buckles dangling from hangers. The back of the closet is thick with dust and cobwebs. It's also very dark. I hit my knee on the edge of something sharp—a trunk, I think—and I jump up and down a little, waiting for the burst of pain to lessen. A cluster of dust gets into my nose and I sneeze and the back of my throat tickles. What in the world am I doing in here, anyway?

Sometimes I seem to move without any purpose to my actions, but something propels me forward. I'm always searching for something even if I don't know quite what.

There's a small box in the corner of the closet; I find it by feel, not sight. I drag it through the mess and emerge from the darkness into the light of the room, pulling it with me. "Ida's Things" is scrawled in thick black marker across the top in Ida's handwriting. Yellowed tape holds down the edges, and without even thinking I pry up the ends with my fingernails and lift off the lid, curious to see what's in here. Perhaps I should feel guilty for journeying into Ida's private things, but my curiosity outweighs my hesitations.

Inside, balls of crumpled old newspaper greet me. I reach in and pull out sheet after crinkly sheet, all bunched up to protect whatever is underneath. My fingers shake with excitement and I feel like a voyeur, discovering some kind of mysterious treasure. The first thing I come to under all the layers is an old black-and-white wedding photograph encased in a gold-edged frame. It's hard to recognize Ida as the young, dewy-faced bride, but there's something the same about her wide smile and the slant of her eyes that confirms this fact for me. She's radiant in her flowing white dress, and the man at her side smiles at her proudly.

I've wondered about the fact that there are no pictures of Ida's husband Stan in the lighthouse. Therefore, this is the first glimpse I've had of the man and he's not at all like I expected. In the old photograph, he's shorter than Ida and very stocky. Even dressed in his tuxedo, with his thinning hair all slicked back from his face, it's clear that he's not a handsome man by conventional standards. His body is too round and he's got a large, bulbous nose, framed by bushy eyebrows that come together to meet at the center of his forehead. But from the way Ida looks at him, her chin tilted slightly down to meet his gaze, he could be a glamorous movie star, a prince, or her knight in shining armor.

Even though the finish of the photo is slightly smudged, it's clear from her expression that she admired him and that he must have felt the same about her. Looking at their young selves standing there on the altar, his hand cupped protectively around her elbow, I know they were truly in love. Things like that you can sense, somehow. Even all these years later, the strength of their love comes shining up through the grainy picture.

This feeling is confirmed even more when I reach farther into the box and remove a slim stack of letters held together with a thin blue ribbon, now fraying at the edges. The letters are all addressed in a sloppy hand to 'Mrs. Stanley Rowan, from Stan.' I take the letters over to the bed and sit there with my back leaning against the headboard to read the messages.

The first letter is dated May 14, 1960, and must have been written shortly after they were married.

My dearest Ida: This is my first time away from you, and I can't wait until we are together again. I miss your sweet face and the way you sleep curled up against me. I will hurry home, my love, as fast as I can. Mother is mending quickly and I should be able to leave in a few days. With loving thoughts of you, your Stan

PS—I am counting down the seconds until I smell your perfume again. Until we are united, I shall look up at the stars every night and comfort myself with the fact that this is the same sky you see, too, my love.

Wow. Jim would never write a letter like that to me. How lucky Ida was to find such a sentimental man.

The next few letters are about everyday stuff that went on over the next ten years. Ida had told me that Stan had left the Coast Guard and gotten a job as a salesman after they were married. He must have traveled a lot in this job, because he wrote from various cities across the country, describing the sights to Ida, who was now at home with their children. I learn from his questions that they had three kids, all close in age, and probably were a handful for Ida. The oldest is Melanie, whom I believe Ida is staying with now. Then there are Jack and Cynthia. Sounds like Ida had her work cut out for her. There's mention of colds and the flu and a fractured arm, birthday parties, a broken lamp, a child with a bad report card. All the types of things you would expect. Then there's a gap of about ten years with no letters. Hmmm. I wonder if Stan didn't travel at all during that time or if Ida simply forgot to save his correspondence during that period.

The next letter is dated Aug. 1, 1980:

Ida: Can you ever forgive me? I suffered a temporary lapse of my senses. You are the only one for me. I still LOVE you, sweetheart, more than ever before. How in the world can I prove it to you?

Your husband, Stan, whose heart is breaking with his own stupidity. It was nothing, I swear to you. PLEASE FORGIVE ME!

I piece together from those words that Stan must have had an affair. Poor Ida. The woman had to deal with betrayal from her one true love.

She and Stan must have made it over this tough time, though, because there's a Valentine's Day card dated the following year, and then random birthday cards all signed simply, *Love, Stan.*

The last piece in the stack is a glossy Valentine's card, one of those commercial ones with the smoky overlay and a big pink heart on the front with a sentimental poem. Inside it bears the date Feb. 14, 2006. This must have been the last card that Stan sent because his death certificate, also in the box, is dated Feb. 28, 2006. Written on the card in a frail script is:

Dear Ida: I love you more today than I ever have before. Each day I feel my love grow so much that my poor heart can barely contain it. Soon I will no longer be here to admire your beautiful face. Have I told you recently how your increasing beauty as you age astonishes me again and again? I love every line on your face and every wrinkle on the back of your hands. I would not trade any of this to have back the young girl you were when we first married. You are tenfold more precious to me now, although I did not think, then, that this would be possible.

I love the woman you have become with a love so deep that at times it has frightened me and led me to do stupid things to prove to myself I wasn't dependent on you for my survival. Believe me, I know only too well that I have not been the perfect husband. Know that I suffer with this knowledge day after day and if I could change things, my dear, I would in a second.

But please feel a sense of pride after I am gone knowing that no woman in this entire world will ever be loved more than you have been by me. We have the last TRUE love, I believe. And when you feel lonely without me, go on down by the ocean on that special beach where we met. I will be waiting for you there, in the Light at Brandypoint Beach, my dear, and we will be together again. With You For Eternity, STAN

I feel tears running down my face as I finish reading this beautiful letter. Despite his possible indiscretions, Stan sounds like he cherished Ida so much. Maybe it takes over forty years of marriage to feel a bond that strong with someone that it could withstand even a betrayal and somehow glue them even more tightly together afterward. I imagine that the love between them is so tangible I feel like it's glowing right here in the room. A deep, solidifying type of love, and very different from the kind of fire Jim and I share.

It's beginning to grow dark outside and reluctantly I pry myself up, stretching my cramping legs, and go over to turn on the lamp on the nearby night table. As I do, I think, yet again, about the fact I haven't heard from Jim in a while. He hasn't responded to my last letter. This realization fills me with a deep sadness and I reach into the box to pull out the last thing in there, a small notebook with a daisy on the cover, then settle myself down against the pillows, eager to delve back into Ida's world.

The cover is stiff when I bend it open, and I smooth it down gently out of the way. Inside are some journal-like entries from Ida. They aren't dated, but I can tell right away that they were obviously all written after Stan's death. There are some heartbreaking notes about how sad she is about Stan's death and how much she misses him. She talks about staying up, sleepless, crying over Stan night after night, and being filled with a desolation so intense that she wonders if she'll be able to go on.

Then she comes up with the idea of moving to the lighthouse, and it's as if her mood lifts right away. There are conversations with the historical society, and details worked out about Ida's selling her house and moving here. Ida is amazed at how smoothly everything falls into place. She says it's like this is all meant to be.

Her last entry is dated in Dec. 2008: It's titled, *Lighthouse*:

Well, I am here at last and with my move comes a sense of peace so deep that I could not have imagined this possible. The house is tiny and filled with Stan's presence. How wonderful it is to be near him again. I have heard lots of people talk about being visited by ghosts in this lighthouse. All sorts of stories have been passed around on the island over the years, but nothing like that has happened to me here. (Although I must admit I would welcome the idea.) Nonetheless, I can see, feel, smell, and hear Stan everywhere. I see him as the young man he was when we met. I was barely 18 at the time, and he had recently turned 20. Then I also can see him as the man he had become in the years and years that we spent together. For a while I didn't know how I would go on. I have enough sleeping pills stored up in the bathroom to kill a body, in case I couldn't spend another minute with this pain. But now that I'm here at the lighthouse, I feel like something has changed, and once again I can go on living. I will always be grateful to this lighthouse for saving me.

The rest of the little notebook is blank.

Chapter 13

While I so envy the love that Ida and Stan shared, I realize that my love for Jim is of a very different nature. Jim and I have always had a strong chemistry between us, ever since that day at the beach when we met all those years ago, even though we didn't act on it right away. But despite the heated passion we share, I don't know if our love is as deep and enduring as Ida and Stan's was. Could I sit home patiently and wait for Jim as he traveled around the way it seems that Stan did? I'm not really sure. In the past, I did wait all those years for Jim to be ready to commit to me, yet now I'm not sure I could wait through something as traumatic again. Yet Ida must have been very secure in their love to stand these absences without losing faith in their marriage. And maybe I'm reading my own interpretation into this and perhaps Ida was really not very patient after all. Obviously, I don't have her responses or know what was going on in her head throughout her marriage. I have only a handful of letters to go by. But based on her journal entries after Stan's death, I imagine that Ida has always loved her husband dearly.

Do I truly love Jim as much? One minute I feel like I can't stand to be without him for another second, and then next thing I know I feel angry and resent him so much. I've never been such a bundle of contradictions before and my swinging moods scare me, making me long to go back to the way I was before Lily. I used to consider myself such a stable person, but suddenly I'm not really sure if this label fits anymore. I wonder if I unexpectedly came across my reflection, would I even recognize myself at all?

I stare at the stack of Stan's letters, which I've placed on Ida's desk, and am filled with longing for the husband and family that Ida had. Despite Stan's apparent lapse and what I assume would be Ida's disappointment and hurt over his betrayal, I like to think they were happy overall. I wish I had some letters like those from Jim to help remind me of all the things that draw us together. My guess is that he would never write anything like that. His letters are much more practical, filled with details about everyday things, not about the sentimental feelings he grapples with. But that's certainly *not* to say that Jim doesn't love me. Although Jim is cold at times, when his love does come out it's all in a rush, like a bubbling river that's getting close to overflowing. Jim likes to live life right in the moment and therefore, I suspect he wouldn't freeze time to reflect and try to capture it in words to savor over later.

I pick up Stan's letters and rest them on my palm, balancing the dry paper and trying to feel the emotion that's caught in the delicate weight of the fibers. Some of the letters are so old that their edges are crumpled and they appear very fragile. Will I look back on Jim's letters, practical as they are, in 40 years to remind myself of this moment?

This question starts me thinking about Jim and reminds me, again, for the millionth time, that I haven't heard from him lately. This thought fills me with a deep weariness, and I set the letters gently back down on the desk and go to bed to rest. My disappointment and discouragement cover me like a blanket and I burrow deeper into the feelings, realizing my hopes of a family have been shattered, and now I'm even questioning the strength of my marriage, leaving little that I can grasp onto to help me feel complete again.

But even as I contemplate all of my failures, I'm suddenly reminded of something I haven't thought about in a while— the morning that Lily was conceived, which was in such a wonderful burst of passion that I find myself falling in love with Jim all over again right now as I replay the scene in my mind. The intensity of the memory suddenly gives me a flicker of hope that maybe my anger with Jim will eventually soften and spread into the quiet kind of love that Stan and Ida shared.

I would have liked to think that Lily was conceived on a beautiful day glowing rich with sunlight. But after checking the dates, I had realized it was much more likely that Lily began on a rainy Sunday morning in the middle of January when Jim and I were too lazy to get out of bed, and something incredible had happened. That morning we had come together with such intensity that it made all our other encounters pale by comparison. And once I discovered this, I knew, rain or not, that Lily was meant to happen.

It was getting late—the clock by the bed read 10 a.m., but the shades were still pulled low so the room had been bathed in darkness. We had been out late last night at a relative's wedding, so even though we had lots to do, neither of us could stand the thought of getting up yet.

I lay there on my stomach, half-awake, hiding my face in my pillow to try to sneak in a few more minutes of sleep. Then Jim stirred beside me, and suddenly there was the warmth of his hand on my leg. I love the way his large palm so easily encircles much of the circumference of my thigh. It makes me feel safe. I reached my fingers down and wrapped them tightly around his wrist, wanting to hold him there forever.

But he moved away, resisting my grasp, and lifted his large body up and over me. Usually we like to hold each other and cuddle before we start fooling around too much, but this time he ignored the formalities. Already I could feel his heat pouring right through me and I shifted under his bulk, trying to get comfortable. He was sweating so hard that splatters of wetness dripped from his bangs onto my cheek and I reached up to wipe the drops off my skin. That's when he grabbed my hand with his and entwined his fingers through mine, lifting my arm high above my head. I had to arch my back a little to keep it there, stretched out like that against the headboard. Then Jim, who often sleeps naked, slowly pushed the sheer fabric of my nightgown aside and gently entered me. I wordlessly pressed my body tighter against him, so I could feel all of him moving inside me. We didn't even kiss. That would have trivialized the force of this moment.

This was such a difference from our earlier days, where Jim and I could hardly tear our mouths apart from each other to take a breath. Kissing then had been one of our favorite things to do together and we never passed up an opportunity for it. This morning, however, there was no need for our lips to even touch; we were so in sync with each other that it didn't even matter. It was as if I couldn't tell where Jim's body left off and mine began, we were so united in every aspect of us. It was a powerful feeling and overwhelming, too. And I think, in that moment, the seeds of Lily were planted.

Afterward, when we breathlessly pulled apart, Jim cradled my head in his arms for a while and stroked my side and I closed my eyes and floated off, more alive than I ever had been, marveling over what had happened between us. This wasn't about sex at all, but rather about feeling so deeply for someone else that I felt like his own blood was coursing through every vein in my body.

We had always been good in bed together, so it was hard to put my finger on exactly what it was that made this encounter so different. But throughout the rest of the day I found myself looking at Jim a little differently, feeling a little closer to him than I ever had before but also seeing him from more of a distance, too, which somehow magnified his presence. I think he looked at me differently, too, as though there was a new and stronger connection between us. That idea reminded me of the night, several years before, when Jim had finally asked me to marry him.

It had been raining then, too, and after he had slipped the ring onto my finger and kissed me to seal the promise of our future, we had looked at each other through new eyes, feeling a strange formality with each other that we hadn't felt in a long time, yet with a special closeness, burning with the knowledge that soon we'd be legally bound together.

After the first few months of our marriage, our love life had seemed to settle into a seamless routine, and sex was always good, always predictable. That's why that morning of wordless passion had been all the more surprising to both of us.

I wonder now, as I lie here in Ida's bed, feeling more alone than ever in the lighthouse without Jim, if Ida and Stan had ever shared the same type of intensity. And how about my parents? They've been married for close to four decades and seem to grow closer with each passing year. They anticipate each other's needs and, much of the time, can even finish each other's sentences. Maybe they're just as in tune with each other in the bedroom, although of course I try not to think about them in that way. At the time that this experience with Jim had happened, I held onto the memory in a selfish way, convinced that no other couple in the world, certainly not my own parents, could have the same feelings as Jim and I did for each other.

Not long after that morning, I noticed a vague tingly warmth flowing lazily through my body and then subtle twinges of something inside that I couldn't describe to the doctor when I saw him several weeks later. But he knew the signs, from my missed period to the bouts of nausea that came on suddenly and then just as quickly subsided. Of course I had wondered, and even hoped, whether this was the start of something new, but I had wanted a baby for so long that I hardly dared think about it for fear I would be disappointed. Even before Jim and I were married I used to hungrily eye infants in their mothers' arms, wondering when I would have one of my own. Jim and I had tentatively talked about having children before, but he always said he wasn't sure if he was cut out to be a father. But despite his hesitation, I had wanted a child desperately. That's why I didn't want to even count on anything until I was sure. I was afraid if I got too excited I might end up jinxing myself in the way that happens to people so often.

So it wasn't until the next day when the nurse called to tell me the news—yes, I really was pregnant—that I even dared to believe it. Then I was happier than I had ever been in my life.

As soon as I got off the phone, I called Jim at work to tell him the good news. I was a little afraid of his reaction at first. I could still hear his words from the last time we had talked about having kids reverberating in my head. "I'm not sure, Claire," he had said yet again. "You know my relationship with my own father was never very good. That's why I'm afraid I don't know how to be a good father myself. I really think we should wait." Now, a few months later, here I was having to tell him that ready or not, here a child was, a tiny fetus maturing inside my stomach with no thought to its father's state of mind.

"Jim, I have something to tell you," I had said, my voice shaking a little. I wondered if he could hear the tremor, or if it was only in my head. Really, I hadn't planned this: I was on the pill, but the doctor had told me that accidents do occasionally happen. But still, would Jim trust me about that? Or would he think I had been skipping doses? Would he be excited or angry? All of these thoughts rushed through my mind, making my hands sweat and my heartbeat go faster.

"Honey, what's wrong?" he asked.

"Are you sitting down?"

"Yeah," he said, but hesitantly. I could hear him making a mental list of all the bad things that could have happened. Was it something with one of my parents, or our friends, or his aunt? I'll bet he was sweating.

"It's nothing bad. In fact, it's actually quite good," I said, wishing I could see his face, stroke his hands in my own, be sure he would be OK with this. Maybe I should wait to tell him until I saw him at home. But I just couldn't keep the secret all to myself.

"What is it?" he asked again.

"It's just that . . . it's that, well, I'm pregnant!"

There was a deep silence, then I could hear Jim laugh. No one was sick or had died. This wasn't something to mourn; it was something to celebrate. He could handle that. He could do this. I could hear him gathering his thoughts to say something nice. Thank God. I said a little prayer in my mind then, not really to my mother's God or anyone specific, but just a general thanks to whoever, or whatever, might be up there, helping me out. I figured no sense taking chances, right?

"Oh, Claire. I didn't expect this, but, but, but . . . well, my God, you're pregnant. We're going to have a baby. I'm going to be a dad. Wow! I can't even believe it! A father. Me. Imagine that!"

I knew, then, that it would be OK. Jim and I were going to be parents and we were going to be great ones. I was still getting used to the fact. I kept stroking my flat stomach and marveling over the idea that there was a baby in there. A real live baby. Our baby.

That night Jim came home with flowers for me. Then he took me to a really expensive Italian restaurant in the North End for a nice dinner and we had a champagne toast to celebrate. This was going to be the last taste of alcohol I would have for the next eight and a half months, so I slowly sipped the fizzy liquid, letting the bubbles melt on my tongue.

"Here's to us," Jim said, clanking glasses with me. We linked our arms together and fed sips to each other, the way we had done on our wedding night. The aroma of tomato sauce and roasting garlic filled the air and wrapped me in a cocoon that felt safe and right.

"Here's to us and to the baby," I said, staring gratefully at Jim's face, at the creases around his eyes, at the tanned line of his neck.

It wasn't until we were home again that Jim cautiously asked the question I had been half-waiting for the whole time, the question I myself had asked. How had this happened if I was on the pill? But when I told him what the doctor had said, he was satisfied with the answer and didn't bring it up again. We both took this as Fate telling us it was time, we were supposed to be parents, and who could argue with that?

From then on we only looked forward, anticipating the birth of our first child.

Chapter 14

Lily Margaret Edwards
Date of birth: Oct. 10th
Time: 12:12 p.m.
Weight: 5 pounds, 9 ounces
Length: 19 inches

This is what Lily's birth announcements would have said if she had lived. When I got home from the hospital, the four packages of blank cards I had bought with such happy anticipation a few weeks earlier were sitting on the dining room table, leering at me. They had a pink background with a stork dangling an infant from its beak. I couldn't bear to see them there, waiting so innocently for me to fill them out and address the envelopes. Jim must have forgotten about them. In a fit of anguish, I ripped the cellophane wrapping from the packs. It made a harsh sound in the silence of the room, causing my ears to ache from the intensity of it.

Once the wrappings were off, I took the 32 cards and carefully fanned them all out on the dining room table, the edges overlapping. Then I grabbed up handfuls of them and tore card after card into little pieces. When I was done, I took the pieces and tore them again, making smaller and smaller shreds, until there was no scrap big enough to show even the eye of a stork or a baby's toe or dimpled finger. I didn't want Jim to see what I had done—he had been so calm and collected through my episodes of raging grief at the hospital—so I found myself scooping up fistfuls of the paper shreds, which looked like confetti, and throwing them into the kitchen sink and flushing the evidence down the disposer.

As I listened to the motor grind away the final traces of those cards, I wished that I could wash away my pain as easily. And thinking about the emotional pain I was in reminded me of the intense physical pain I had endured during labor, birthing Lily.

I felt the first pains of labor before dawn on Monday morning. I lay on my side of the bed, heavy with the baby's form, my knees pulled up as high as they'd bend. I knew right away what the pain meant. Jim was asleep beside me. The baby wasn't formally due for another two weeks, but ready or not, here she was. I didn't wake Jim right away. I lay still, getting used to the feeling that ran across my middle and left me breathless. I knew, from the Lamaze class we had taken together, that it would be hours before the baby appeared.

With the second pain, which came close to 20 minutes later, I gently shook Jim by the shoulder and instantly he was awake and ready for action. Our car was in a parking garage several blocks away, so he called a cab and we rushed to the hospital, but it wasn't until 10 a.m., long after my water had broken, that I went into full labor.

When the pain became too much for me to bear, the nurse gave me a shot of Demerol. At first the medicine gave me a rush of relief, which helped me escape from the heaviness of my body and the stabbing cramps that filled every inch of me. I felt myself floating up and over the sterile room, peering down upon Jim's bowed head and the monitor, which stood next to my bed drawing the shape of my pain in lines on a glowing machine for all to see.

But then the pain came back in full force and I found myself on the delivery room table, my legs spread wide in cold metal stirrups that threatened to split me in half, if the labor didn't do it first.

Jim's white face, anxiously close beside mine, seemed hazy and unfamiliar. It was hard to focus, with the deep, sharp pain pulsing through my body and taking over. It was hard to think. I concentrated on a glow of light from the ceiling; the gleaming coats of white paint; the way the edge of Jim's nails felt pressing against my clenched fists; and how the doctor's face looked like a mountain, framed in the valley of my knees. Rivers of sweat flowed down my body, drenching me in wetness. And still the pain relentlessly gripped me sucking me in, filling me until I feared I would be swallowed up by its intensity. Then I was sinking into the table, unable to float up to the surface and gasp breaths of clean, fresh air. I felt myself drowning.

Suddenly, lying on the table, I understood the full impact of what pain meant and realized that the other women I'd talked to had not told me even the half of it. As the baby's head began to crown, I called to the doctor to stop the delivery. I didn't want to have a baby after all. Jim laughed, even though I could tell he was tense, and I released my iron grip on his hand long enough to slap ineffectually at him.

But through my tears and the warmth of Jim's hand, at the very instant when I thought I couldn't bear this any longer, I suddenly saw a flash of light in the operating room and an old memory, long forgotten, came to me.

In the memory, I was five or six years old and had fallen down in the playground when I was visiting my grandmother, who died many years ago.

I clearly remembered how the rough pavement had felt when I fell, biting into the fragile curve of my little knee, and the way the skin had split open and a gush of blood quickly stained my new white tights with ugly smudges. I had sat there, right on the dirty ground amid dented soda cans and crumpled candy wrappers and puddles, and fiercely hugged my legs to my chest, staring down at the open wound, tears streaming down my cheeks, afraid I was dying.

Then my grandmother had slowly made her way over, leaning heavily on her wooden cane. "You'll be OK, Claire," she had said, helping me back to my feet and hugging my small body tightly against her larger one. She didn't seem to care if any of the blood rubbed onto her.

Lying on the table, I remembered the gentle touch of my grandmother's hand, how her palm had felt soft even as the rest of her skin was old and crinkly. With this image firmly in my mind, I felt a new force clamping down on me, struggling to break free. The pressure of the baby trying to be born, ready to begin a new life, even as I was thinking of an old one.

The evening of Lily's birth, Jim and I celebrated with a toast of sparkling cranberry seltzer water in our best crystal glasses he had brought from home. (Sometimes he surprises me and *can* be romantic.) He had also brought two bouquets of flowers, one of red roses for me and tiny pink ones for the baby. They both sat in vases on the bedside table, filling the room with their sweet scent.

I thought the baby looked exactly like Jim and he thought she looked like me. We had a new bond now that we had gone through the experience of birthing a child together. Even though I had done all the work, he had stood beside me and supported me over the rough moments. That was what really mattered. And I felt like our relationship was tied together with a ribbon of security that was missing before. Until then, we had been bound only by our vows and the marriage certificate we kept in our night table drawer. But after the birth, I reveled in the knowledge that this baby would link us together for life. And thinking of that reminded me: where was the baby?

"I want Lily here with me," I said crankily, still feeling the after-effects of the birthing process. There was lots of pain and lots of soreness, but I knew it was all worth it. I had already seen the baby four times in the eight hours since she had been born, but I hadn't tried to breastfeed her yet. I was too weak from the labor to do that and the nurse told me to wait until I felt stronger, since she could supplement with bottles of formula. Now, I was finally ready and the baby wasn't in the room. Jim told me she would be back soon but I felt impatient and didn't want to wait. She was my baby and I wanted her here with me. I missed her already. This feeling that I felt for her was different from anything I had known before. It came with a fierceness that was scary but invigorating.

Then the nurse came back, carrying Lily, swaddled in a pale pink receiving blanket, and laid her in my arms. She snuggled against me, her lips sucking the air, telling me she was hungry. Gingerly, I pushed open the front of my nightgown. She couldn't seem to find the tip of my breast and Jim watched, amused, as I tried to guide her to the right spot. She kept turning her head away, squirming, refusing to take the nipple between her lips. This went on and on for a long time. Frustrated, I started to cry.

"Here, let me help," Jim said, coming over to the bed and directing the baby's face to where the nipple sprang, taut and pink. He moved her mouth to the right spot until her tiny round lips parted to catch onto the nipple. Then she began to suck.

A warm, tingling feeling began in my breast then radiated in little lines up and down my whole body. The feeling reminded me of the heat of an orgasm, but there was also an added depth and fire.

I could feel Jim still standing beside us as I relaxed into the moment, and I wondered if he envied the bond I had already created with our child throughout the long pregnancy and now, through our very first feeding session.

When Lily grew tired of the sucking motion, the intensity of her pulls lessened. I perched her against my shoulder to burp her, and she suddenly felt so still and light, almost motionless. I wondered if she could be asleep. I lowered her so I could look at her face and I saw how white and thin she seemed, such a change from the vivacious little infant I had just been feeding seconds earlier. Something felt very different.

"Jim, Jim," I cried, my voice a loud slash of color against the whiteness of the hospital room. Jim took one look at me and the baby's pale stillness, then added his frantic voice to mine, calling for a nurse, a doctor, anyone who could help us.

They were there in seconds, white coats pulling my baby out of my arms, working over her still, silent form. Jim was beside me the whole time, gripping my hand more tightly than anything I had ever felt. In his other hand, he squeezed the crystal wine glass, squeezed it so hard that he snapped the fragile stem in half. Its sharp edge sliced his finger and made it bleed, but neither of us noticed then, even as his shirt and the floor beneath him became spotted with red streaks.

When our daughter died moments later—from what we later learned was a congenital heart defect—the light went out of the room. But I could feel her spirit lifting over me, floating up toward the ceiling, or maybe higher, out of my reach. Then, abruptly, her essence drained from the room.

Suddenly, I was left feeling more alone than I ever had been before, even in the midst of all the hospital staff still hovering around Lily's still form.

Chapter 15

Now Lily is back with me, back in the only way she can be. I sit outside on the hard-packed surface of sand a few feet away from the lighthouse and stare out at the layers of blue and green waves that make up the ocean. Lily's ghost lies beside me, snugly wrapped in her white blanket. It's pretty warm today—I wear only a thick fisherman's sweater, no coat—yet I can see the motion of my breath stain the clearness of the air, providing a sharp contrast to Lily's stillness.

I gently run my fingers along her smooth cheek, memorizing the way it feels. This reminds me of another time, when I had touched Lily's skin in the funeral home, shrinking back from the coolness of death and the rigidity of her delicate skin. Now, though, her cheek feels like air, a whispery touch, with nothing solid beneath it. The sun is so bright that I have to squint in order to see the top of the lighthouse tower. With the wisps of clouds arched behind it, the scene is like a postcard photograph, surreal in its beauty.

I remember when Jim and I had first met here, how we had marveled then, too, about the lighthouse's magnificent presence. What a long time ago that was. I ponder over the way things have changed over the course of years. Yet somehow the lighthouse has remained exactly the same.

I wanted so badly in those early days, and even later, for Jim to marry me. I had imagined the children we would have, and could even see glimpses of them when I looked at Jim in a certain way, catching him at just the right angle. I would be filled with an image of our child toddling along beside him, his or her tiny hand wrapped inside Jim's large one. But I never told Jim my fantasies, knowing he wouldn't appreciate them. Jim has always held a part of himself back, never letting himself get too wrapped up in anything.

Throughout my uneven relationship with Jim, I've always struggled with the fact that he has two distinct sides that often are at odds with each other. One half of Jim strongly longs to love and be loved, and yet the other half feels claustrophobic when those needs are satisfied, causing him to retreat in silence from the very thing he had originally gone after. This has always been a source of deep frustration for me.

I think about this paradox as I stare at Lily's form.

"I love you Lily, I love you, my sweet," I whisper to her.

"I love you, momma," she answers back, just as I knew she would.

It was a torturous four years after Jim and I met before we actually started dating. Until then, we had stayed in touch and even saw each other occasionally, but I always had to suffer through stories of his latest girlfriends and all the wonderful things they did together. I dated others, too, but found myself always comparing the other men to Jim, always looking for slivers of him in other faces. It's amazing how in a crowd, the curve of a cheek, the wave of hair, or the boldness of a hand can remind you of someone else entirely.

I could not put my finger on exactly what it was about Jim that had attracted me to him. Nonetheless, I found myself showing him parts of myself that, to the rest of the world, remained hidden. For instance, I would share with him things that others would simply laugh at. Like my dream when I was 10 to run away and become a tightrope walker in the circus, wearing those fancy costumes that glittered with each step. And how, in my early teens, I had fantasized about moving to Lancaster, Pennsylvania, and becoming Amish, to wear those stark dark dresses with white aprons and simple white cloth bonnets. Jim had never looked surprised at any of my confessions, but instead listened seriously to whatever I said, reflecting on my words for a moment and then asking me questions. It was like he accepted me with all of my eccentricities and I accepted him back, allowing him his more rigid way of showing affection without belittling him. He, too, found himself showing hidden sides of himself to me that other women didn't tap into. He would spend time patiently studying my paintings and exploring the brush strokes and the way the colors blended together. I think he also liked the ease that accompanied our interactions and how easily he, who hated to talk on the phone, could babble away with me for hours.

But nothing more, until a fateful Tuesday night when our friendship took a new direction. Afterward, he was left unsure of how to cope with the change, and so, in his usual fashion, he retreated in silence. I think he hoped things would return to normal on their own.

That Tuesday night when everything changed, the city had been in the throes of a horrible heat wave that made the sidewalk steam and left people listless and edgy. There was no air to be found anywhere.

Jim and I sat at an outdoor café on Newbury Street, fanning ourselves with our hands, thirstily gulping glasses of water. We had finished dinner a while ago, but neither of us had the will or the strength to leave. Finally, Jim forced himself to get up from his seat, wiping ineffectively at a line of sweat that trickled down his forehead. Then he offered his hand to help me get up.

I took his fingers in mine and a sharp current of electricity ran between us. The intensity of the feeling shook us both. We stood there for a moment, both afraid to speak, not wanting to ruin the magic of this encounter.

"I feel like walking around for a bit, how about you?" I finally asked.

"Sure," Jim said.

We strolled casually up and down the crowded street, without really having any destination. We lingered here and there to look at the glossy displays set up in store windows. But even pressing my face up to the glass to stare at the mannequins adorned in fancy clothes and jewelry, I didn't really see anything. My mind and pulse raced with Jim standing so close beside me. The heat emanating from him quivered in the heavy air, stealing my breath right out of my chest.

Later, Jim walked me the twenty or so blocks to my apartment. We sauntered along in silence, listening to the noises of the city swirl around us. The whole way home I agonized over whether to invite him in or not. But I needn't have wondered over this. When we got to my apartment building, Jim held the front door open then followed quickly after me. He escorted me up the four flights of stairs, not saying anything. As soon as my door closed, locking us away from the rest of the world, his lips found mine and stayed there.

He spent the night in my narrow bed, sweat gluing our bodies together. I reveled in a burst of happiness that Jim had finally, finally, after all this time, come to realize that he had feelings for me. For years I had imagined this scene, and now that the moment was here, it was every bit as wonderful as I had known it would be. Jim didn't say that he loved me at any point, but I knew that he did. I could read the words on his face and in the tender way that he gazed at me.

After kissing for hours, mindless of the stifling heat in the room, we finally made love for the first time as the weak rays of early morning sun filled the room. Although we were shy with each other and a little tentative, the experience was incredible.

I woke to the comfort of Jim snuggling against me. Even before I opened my eyes I could feel his warmth, and the reality of the night came back to me in a rush. Lying there, I smiled at the memory of our joined bodies and luxuriated in the hardness of his arm perched behind my neck, even though after a while it began to dig into my skin and make my muscles ache. But I didn't want to move and disturb him. In sleep, the tension usually apparent on his face was smoothed out, leaving him looking innocent and sweet as a child. I ran my feet over the soft, but bristly, texture of his skin.

Jim woke soon after I did, returning to the world slowly, moving his legs gingerly in the cramped space of my bed as he tried to get his bearings. When he was fully awake and realized what we had done, he rested his hand on top of my head, stroking through my silky hair, probably trying to comprehend how this could have happened. Then, instead of kissing me as I had expected, he turned his face away, unable to look at me.

A burst of pain filled me and I pulled the sheet tightly around my bare body, wanting to hide myself from him. We both got up and dressed in silence, then ate a stilted breakfast together before he left. But his silence filled the room like a physical presence. He didn't call again.

When weeks passed, I tried to contact him myself. I was so angry and hurt that he could have used me like this, and

I wanted to talk to him about it. Even though I should have known this was Jim's 'way,' and in fact, I probably should have expected his response, that knowledge didn't make me feel any better. He wouldn't take my calls at the law firm where he worked. And when I reached him at home in the evenings, he'd say he was busy and had to go. Then he would hang up, leaving me holding the phone in my hand, the dial tone buzzing insistently as the tears streamed down my face. Sometimes I really hated him.

For months I suffered from an anguish deeper than any I'd ever known. I'd broken up with boyfriends before, and I'd been dumped, too. I also suffered through several one-night stands, but none of those experiences had prepared me for this. Not only did I feel horrible about the circumstances, but I also dearly missed the friendship we had shared. I was hurt and embarrassed and bewildered that Jim, my friend, could have treated me so cruelly. Night after night I lay awake, thinking about this, staring at the ceiling, catching traces of Jim's cologne still on my sheets, even though I had washed them dozens of time. Still, his presence refused to be erased.

I found that because of this experience, I had changed. Before that night, I used to enjoy spending time by myself, taking a walk down Charles Street to wander through the antiques shops or renting old movies I loved to play on the DVD player in my living room. But suddenly, thoughts of Jim were too big for my head and I found myself trying to shrink his image down with new pictures of other men, trying to cram my world full of noise to drown out his silence. I couldn't stand to be alone, so I started seeking out friends I hadn't seen in a while, accepting dates with men I didn't even find attractive, anything to put Jim behind me. But, leaning my head against someone else's arm, I felt more alone than ever. And when another man rubbed my back and held me, Jim's face flooded over his features, transposing himself there, so it was really Jim I was kissing. There were lots of men and lots of fun, but I couldn't sleep with any of them. Jim was the one I wanted.

Then fate intervened. We bumped each other again several months later, at a friend's party. I hadn't known Jim was going to be there.

The party was well under way when I got there. I entered the living room, where most of the guests were gathered, and instantly braced myself. There was an onslaught of noise, smoke, and commotion, which turned the air into a hazy, heavy hot curtain spread out over everyone. The sticky pungent smell of keg beer was overwhelming. Someone handed me a red plastic cup and I took a deep sip, savoring the coolness of the liquid even as I tried to avoid the foam that collected on the top. I had come with my friend Sonja but now I had lost her, and I scanned the crowd, seeking other faces that I knew.

There was one that looked suspiciously familiar and my eyes caught on the sight, refusing to let go. Could that be Jim? I wondered. From the side, the man looked like him, but then lately everyone looked like him. It was probably someone else, someone who didn't even resemble him. My mind had been playing tricks on me so much that I couldn't trust my vision anymore when it came to this.

Then he turned to face me and I could see his eyes and the shape of his hair, which looked the same as I remembered, yet even more so. Jim, in person, had more Jimness to him than the one in my mind. It was easy to see that, now, with the real thing standing larger than life in front of me. Making me ache and tingle all over, even as I told myself it was useless and to forget about him—now.

But that was easier said than done. There was a dark edge that defined him for me, making it impossible for me to lose sight of him, no matter where he wandered throughout the room.

Finally, he made his way over, hesitant and maybe a little nervous, but determined to do the 'right' thing, whatever that was. Up close, his eyes were brighter and clearer than I had ever seen. I felt almost hypnotized by the deep turquoise color.

"Hey," he said, holding his beer loosely in his hand. I sensed that he was waiting—he even cringed a little—for me to yell at him.

"Hi," I said softly, narrowing my gaze at him. There seemed to be a magnet there that glued our faces together. I couldn't break its pull no matter how hard I tried. Or maybe I just didn't try hard enough.

"What's up?" he asked. That was all. But those simple words brought back all those days and nights we had talked on the phone. In those simple words I remembered, yet again, how much I missed Jim.

"Not much," I said, and paused, letting him know without words that I wouldn't berate him for his actions. I knew Jim was aware that he had treated me badly and he had his own conscience to live with, which would punish him more thoroughly than anything I could say to him.

"How's your painting coming?" he asked.

"It's great!" I was happy to stand there, in the midst of all of the people, and describe to Jim the latest project I was working on. How I was trying to capture the play of light on a vase of water that was set up in front of my window. How the glass reflected the sun's rays and turned them into slivers of light in some places, curves of dark in others. His eyes lit up as I verbally painted the scene for him.

"Maybe you could show me," he said. "I'd sure love to see it for myself."

"Sure," I said. "Sure!"

The next night he dropped by to see the painting, which he loved, and then took me to dinner. I figured he at least owed me a meal as a peace offering for all the heartache he had caused. But I knew, even as I played with that thought, that I was just rationalizing my acceptance of his behavior. The truth was that I wanted to see what would happen next. I couldn't change the past but wanted to see what the future held in store for us. In those months without Jim's friendship, I had missed him so much that I couldn't bear *not* to try again. I felt somehow like I was *supposed* to be with Jim. As though it was fate or part of some bigger plan that I couldn't fight, nor did I want to.

Over the next few weeks, we began to date, always with me initiating. Dinner, movies, watching TV. Jim was a wary participant, but he made sure to keep things a little strained so I didn't get too comfortable. And we didn't sleep together again. He said that we should take things slowly and see what happened. I was just so happy to be with Jim again that I let him set the pace he wanted, although I tried, time and again, to see if I could speed him up a little, but to no avail. Jim wouldn't let me push him into anything. Romantic dinners at my house made him scared, and he would always leave right after we ate, afraid he would get carried away and sleep with me again and then I would expect something. And I sent him funny cards and gave him cute little gifts to make him appreciate me more, all of which he ignored.

Whenever I went too far, he would pull back. He would ignore my calls again for a few days or a week, playing hard-to-get. But then a week later he would mellow and be more receptive to me, and we would slowly progress back to our dating routine, but each time a step behind where we had been the time before. The whole frustrating routine was driving me crazy. Yet I couldn't quit.

"I love your father and always have," I whisper to the sleeping Lily as she stretches in her sleep. I like to imagine she's smiling at the words, even though I know she's really too young to understand what they mean. It's getting colder now, as the afternoon lengthens on toward evening. The sand takes on new hazy layers in the deepening shadows. Lily's face, too, takes on an iridescent cast, like the underside of a shell, with that milky sheen that's slippery to the touch.

This has been such a nice day relaxing here with my baby and reliving my past in scene after scene. I have a faint hope that in the process, I'll be able to figure out more what it all means.

I remember how much I loved Jim all those years ago, but I couldn't tell him how I felt back then. He certainly didn't want to hear it. Instead, I would practice whispering the words into the weight of my pillowcase at night, letting them stay trapped there, imagining that Jim lay beside me and could hear. I felt daring and yet scared to say those words, even though I was alone and there was no one to know. Yet I was half afraid that once spoken, the sounds would escape from the pillowcase and break free, seeping right through my walls, right through the city, floating their way across the miles to Jim's room. It was a full five years since Jim and I had met that day at the beach before I finally worked up the nerve to tell him how much I cared about him.

It was a late spring night the first time I told Jim I loved him. By then we had already been dating off and on for nearly a year, but it was not a steady thing and often I didn't know on the weekends if I would even see Jim. He made it clear I shouldn't count on him for anything. He was still dating other people, too, and he made sure I knew it. He would drop little hints (never coming out and telling me straight, of course), wanting to be sure I didn't feel too secure with him. Out of self-defense I followed suit, accepting random dates when I had a chance. I was frustrated that I was no further

along with Jim than I had been when we were 'just friends.'
I kept waiting, hoping that soon he would want more. I kept
thinking it was just a matter of time, but eventually he would
get it. In the meantime, I existed in fear, waiting for Jim to
spoil everything by telling me that he didn't want to see me
again.

There was such a clear pattern in our interactions, yet
Jim simply couldn't see it. Whenever the relationship started
to feel too intense for him, he would end things. I would be
devastated and hurt and I would cry for a few weeks and
nurse my wounds, and find that I couldn't stop thinking
about him.

Each time, when I couldn't get him out of my mind, I
would work up the nerve to call him and ask if we could at
least still be friends. He would always be pleased to hear
from me. Then we would start from scratch as though we
were acquaintances, slowly working our way back into
dating again.

I had a perpetual stomach ache keeping me up most
nights, and I took turns being sad because Jim had dumped
me again, excited because we had decided to give it another
shot, or worried because even though we were trying, I knew,
ultimately, he would break up with me in the end.

Every time we seemed to find a steady pace and rhythm
for our interactions, giving me hope that the relationship
would eventually progress into something more, something
I could count on, Jim would call it quits. It seemed to me that
as soon as his feelings started to get out of control, he became
overwhelmed and had to run from them. After a while, I
could feel myself wilting under Jim's constant assaults. Was
any man worth this? I wondered.

"Yes," Lily tells me. "Yes, momma. Aren't I worth it?
Aren't I, mommma?"

"Of course, my sweet, of course you are. Yes. Yes. Yes."

Lily has just woken up from her nap and I can see as she shifts on the blanket how much she looks like Jim.

The last time Jim broke up with me, we were sitting in my living room having a beer. We had just come back from dinner and I noticed Jim had been quiet all night.

"Are you OK?" I asked, resting my hand on his back. He looked a little pale and I was afraid he was working too hard and getting run down. Maybe he was getting sick.

"Well, there's something I have to tell you, Claire." Jim glanced at me, then down at his hands, then back at me again. His eyes were such a brilliant flash of light in the room, I knew this was going to be something big.

"What's wrong?" I asked, even though part of me already knew. As I had played with my chicken and rice at the restaurant a few hours ago, explaining that my stomach felt funny and I couldn't seem to eat, I must have intuitively felt the curtain lowering to darken my hopes once again, just like last time.

"This just isn't working," Jim said, shaking his head and gazing at me sorrowfully.

"Not again!" I cried. My heart was in my throat and I suddenly felt very old. But I was determined not to let myself go. I usually was able to hold back the tears until after Jim had gone.

"I'm sorry," Jim said, pulling my shaking body to him, hugging me tightly to his chest. Then he started to kiss me.

I kissed him back with all my strength, hoping that the depth of my feelings would transfer from my lips to his and make him stay.

"Please don't do this, Jim," I said, recognizing the words I had said before—was it four times or five by now that we had played out this scene? In my anguish, I couldn't remember. All I knew was that the pain got worse with each round.

"I'm sorry," he said again miserably, his eyes growing brighter and sharper by the second. "I just don't seem to have the right feelings for you. You need to find someone who does, someone who'll marry you."

But even as the hurtful words sprang across the room, I didn't believe them. I couldn't. I loved Jim so much. He was mindlessly stroking the fabric of my skirt with his hands, looking deeply into my eyes, telling me with his face that he loved me. He did, that was why he was doing this. He loved me so much he had to leave me and get away; it was so scary for him.

What an ironic way life had, I thought, as I laid my cold hand on the warmth of his palm and wished I could freeze him there. It felt so right to be sitting here together. Nothing I had ever felt before could begin to equal the feelings I had with him. Didn't he feel it too?

But whether he felt it or not, he wouldn't stay. He was up and moving away, leaving the room, going into the kitchen. My whole world suddenly seemed to stop, and time turned into slow motion and sounds. *Tap*: the sound of his footsteps, which drowned out my pulse pounding in my ears. *Clink*: the sound of him putting his beer bottle in the sink. *Swish*: the noise of him getting his windbreaker, putting it on. *Zippp*: there, he was done. Ready to go out into the night. Escape, move far away from me. Leave me far behind. He couldn't get away fast enough.

I stayed in my spot on the couch, listening to the sounds of him collecting his things, getting ready to leave. The man I loved was getting away once again. I always knew it would end. But I couldn't believe it.

"I'm really sorry," he said again, his voice soft and smooth in the room, hanging there in the air.

I felt like I could see the words burned in front of me. "I love you, Jim," I said then, surprising myself that I had let the secret out so easily.

"I know you do."

Next thing I knew, he was gone. The door made a soft thud when he closed it behind him.

"For months after that, Jim and I barely talked to each other." I tell Lily this, watching how her blue eyes shine in the sunlight. Their color is almost as brilliant as Jim's are. I lean down and kiss her cool forehead, breathing in her baby scent.

"What happened, momma? What happened to you both?" Lily asks me, her voice singing out in the freshness of the beach like beautiful music.

"Don't worry, my sweet little baby, your father and I did work things out," I tell her, stroking her tiny arm. My words swirl around her in the air, like a lullaby or a child's song. Her breathing becomes slow and even, matching her rhythm to my sound.

"I would call your daddy once in a while to say hello, but I was through scheming little ways to make him wake up and realize he loved me," I tell Lily now.

I had resigned myself to the fact that Jim and I just weren't meant to be. All of my earlier instincts had been wrong and so I tried to block him out of my mind and focus strictly on my own survival. I had no time left for Jim. He had beaten all the life out of me and I needed to be alone just to try to recover. In my mind, I tried to forgive him for being so cruel and I truly wished him well, though not without an addendum: I hoped that I would meet someone new first and be completely happy myself before he was.

I try to keep the words soft and even, to comfort Lily, not to alarm her. I realize she doesn't know what anything means, but still I feel the need to share these things.

I especially want to tell her the best part, which is what everything that had come before was leading to: the night Jim miraculously came to his senses. Lily's face seems to brighten. She must hear in my voice the lively tone, the fact that this is the highlight of everything.

It was just after midnight on a September night and I was sitting in my living room painting my nails. The rain drummed against the outside of my apartment loudly, echoing in the stillness of the room. My stereo was on, but I had to keep the volume down low so I didn't disturb my neighbors; I could barely hear the music over the loudness of the storm.

My apartment seemed a little eerie at this time of night, and I imagined I was on a ship, sailing off somewhere alone. I kind of liked this idea. It gave a romantic twist to the real truth, which was simply that I was lonely.

When my doorbell rang, I jumped, startled. (No one except Jim ever stopped by unannounced and it couldn't be him.) People in the city always called first, even in the daytime, to see if it was a convenient time for a visit. But it couldn't be Jim, because he hadn't been by in months. Yet even with this thought, I could feel my heart racing in excitement, hoping against hope it was him. I wanted to see him so badly. Even though I was over him, I willed his name out of my mind, refusing to let myself even go there now. Why was this man so hard to forget? I wondered for the umpteenth time.

"Who is it?" I called through the speaker that rang out onto the street.

"Jim."

"Jim?" *Oh, no.* Jim? It was Jim. How could it be him? I wondered if I could have fallen asleep and didn't know it.

Even though during the day I tried to control my thoughts to keep Jim out, at night he flowed through all of my dreams, so maybe this was one of them. In the sleeping hours between midnight and dawn, I could see him, taste his skin, smell his cologne, talk to him. That's why it was always a disappointment when I woke to the sound of my alarm in the morning and realized I was alone. But this wasn't a dream; this was real life. In a daze, I pushed the buzzer to let him in. I missed him so terribly. Even when I wasn't thinking about it, his name lay heavy inside me, like a headache that you had for so long you barely noticed it anymore.

Seconds later, Jim was there, rain dripping off his hair, his jacket, his face. He looked so beautiful, standing before me. I had forgotten how tall he was.

"Hey," he said.

I looked at him deeply, questioningly, wondering what to say. It took all my self-control not to throw myself into his arms and breathe in his familiar scent, but I held myself back, unsure of what he wanted from me. I wouldn't make this easy for him.

"Listen, I've been thinking, Claire." His words raced out one on top of the other, jumbling together in his haste. "Since we've been apart, well, I realize, I realize I miss you."

Oh, my God. I had imagined him saying the words for so long, yet this couldn't be real. Maybe I was dreaming after all. And yet, even as I tried to figure this out, tried to connect this scene into the reality of my lonely life, there was a part of me that felt calm and right, as though I had been waiting all along and knew, of course, that this was supposed to happen. Of course Jim would be here saying this. How could I have given up that hope? I had known it all along but had just not been sure when.

Then Jim reached out and pulled me into his arms and I rested my head against the wetness of his jacket, not even minding that the water soaked my sweatshirt. The cold felt good against my burning skin.

"Oh, Jim." I knew I shouldn't get caught up in it again. Jim was no good for me. My family and friends told me that all the time, despite the fact that they really did like him. But they knew what I refused to admit: this man just couldn't seem to commit to a real relationship.

Even as these thoughts whirled through my mind, I could hear Jim's voice, so near and real and dear to me.

"Everywhere I go, there are things that've been making me think of you. I see reminders of the beach everywhere. I even dream about you now," he said. "You're driving me crazy and I need to be with you."

The words set my head spinning in circles so fast that the rug shifted beneath my feet and I stretched out my hand to rest against his arm, needing an anchor to assure me that this was real and to keep me from casting off.

Then he was reaching into his pocket and was pulling something out. I craned my head to see what it was. His fingers fumbled with a little dark blue box and even as my mind registered what it was, I refused to believe it. I couldn't stand to be disappointed again. Then he flicked open the top and there it was, a diamond ring. An engagement ring. I started to cry, I was so happy and I had wanted this for so long and had even given up hoping anymore, it seemed so impossible.

"I love you," he said, the words sounding so familiar in the warmth of my hallway, even though I had never heard them before, not from Jim's beautiful voice, and I focused on the gleam that filled his eyes, and the way he stepped closer and closer to me, twisting his fingers impatiently, eagerly, through my hair. His lips found mine and he kissed me.

Later, when we came up for air, he slipped the ring on my finger and said the words I had been waiting for my whole life. I had always wanted this moment to happen, probably even before I was born.

"Claire, will you marry me?"

The ring flashes on my finger just as prettily now as it did back then. Now I have a sparkling wedding band to go with it, too, and I hold out my hand to show Lily both. Her little eyes follow the way the light shines off the stones, transfixed by the glint.

I remember how in the first few weeks of being engaged, I had spent so much time staring at the ring, turning it different angles to see it better, moving my hand in wide sweeps, hoping others would notice it, too. I was so proud. I would cup my right palm over the top of the stone, noticing how cool and strong the surface felt. A tangible reminder that Jim was now mine. I wore the ring all the time, even to sleep, often waking myself up during the night just to make sure the diamond was still there. I would finger the curve of the stone and breathe a sigh of relief, then, satisfied, I'd drift back off into the warm, cushiony layers of sleep.

But even with the weight of these rings resting on my finger, I realize now that I've never quite felt secure in my marriage. There was so much waiting and frustration and turmoil that had come before, that the memory of these things keeps me poised as if I hang onto the edge of some kind of cliff and any false move could make me tumble headfirst to the bottom.

It's so hard to see this threat when I'm with Jim. Then it's just so integrated inside of me that I barely notice it. I move around the edges, never looking down, but always careful to avoid the slippery spots. Now, though, reflecting back on my life from the safety of the lighthouse, I can see things more clearly. I know that throughout our marriage, Jim has continued to deal the way that he did in the past, pulling back into one of his silences whenever he needs to escape from our emotional intimacy. That really hurts me a lot, and makes me feel afraid he'll eventually leave me. Maybe that's why I left him first.

I also think that some of my insecurity stems from the fact that I've never fully understood what it was that convinced Jim that he loved me and wanted to marry me. I've asked him time and time again, but he never has an answer. He just says, in his vague way, that one morning he woke up with me on his mind and I lingered with him throughout the day and he found he couldn't shake me. Sometimes I worry that, just as suddenly, he'll wake up and realize he's made a mistake.

"Good night, mommy," Lily says, her voice jerking me back to the beach.

"Good night, little precious baby," I reply, kissing her cheek, watching as her delicate eyes softly close and her little face relaxes as she drifts off to sleep. She breathes so evenly, deeply, her chest fluttering with each beat. I lie down beside her, spreading out on the coldness of the sand. And as I do, the silences seem to hover above me, above both of us, so close that I believe I can reach out and touch their jagged textures. I wonder, then, if all of this time I have secretly held on to my resentment of Jim. Could it be that I've never quite forgiven him for everything?

This question forces me to sit back up abruptly, shaking the hard granules of sand from the strands of my hair where they linger. I wonder if I could have left Jim to punish him for all the different silences that have come between us, and to make him suffer the way he's made me suffer over time. Maybe coming here to the lighthouse is *my* way of enforcing my own kind of silence.

Chapter 16

I used the last of the milk on my cereal this morning, so after lunch I decide to go to the market and pick up some more. I walk slowly along the edge of the road, drifting off in my thoughts as I go, in no rush to arrive at my destination. These days the process seems more important than the end result. But the fresh air clears a path through the heavy curtain of thoughts that make me feel slightly dizzy and unreal sometimes when I'm alone inside the lighthouse.

Outside, the brightness of the sky and the firmness of the ground provide a reminder of the things I used to take for granted before Lily was even an idea in my mind.

My thoughts are interrupted when a wet slap across my cheek startles me. Then comes a splatter of mud on my navy pants. I look up in dismay to see a dusty red Toyota whizzing past, dislodging the melting ice puddles in the road.

"Damn!" I jump back onto the grass, dropping my purse down onto the ground. Lily is not with me today, so I don't have to worry about holding her. With two hands free, I can concentrate as I swipe at the stain, which looks like it's setting deeper with every passing second. So much for shopping, I guess. I'll need to go home and change into dry clothes.

As I bend over to pick up the purse, the Toyota screeches to a halt and then backs up. The door creaks open and there's the soft slap of shoes against the pavement as the driver rushes over.

"Claire! I'm so sorry about that. Here, take a tissue and see if those spots will come off."

At the sound of Diana's voice, I whip my head up, startled to see her wide, friendly face and those very blue eyes again. She smiles apologetically and hands me a cluster of Kleenex, then helps me rub at the wet area, trying in vain to remove the mud spot.

"My fault," she says. "I was driving so fast, I didn't even see that puddle."

"That's OK. I'm sure the dry cleaner will be able to save the pants," I say, shrugging as I give up. "If not, it's really no big deal. This is an old pair, anyway. Comfortable, though, so I haven't wanted to throw them away." Yet even as I say this, I remember wearing the pants when I was first pregnant with Lily. They were one of my few articles of stretchy clothing that fit as I began to get larger. I rest my hands on my stomach now, feeling empty at the smoothness of it, missing the hills of Lily's head, her bottom, all scrunched up inside of me.

"Yes," Diana says, tugging at the elastic waistband of her own pants. "I know what you mean. Some of my favorite clothes are the ones I've had for a while, the ones that feel like I'm wearing pajamas when I put them on." She stretches one leg to show me where the cotton is faintly wearing through. "But they feel so nice on, I can't give them up. They're perfect around the house, especially since Sophia doesn't see so well. She's a fussy one all right, but she doesn't know the difference, anyway."

"Where is Sophia? And Carlo?" I ask.

"Sophia's daughter is here today to take her to a doctor's appointment. On the way home she's picking up Carlo from school." She glances at her watch.

"Hey, I've still got an hour until three and I've finished everything. I'm about to go home and brew some tea. Why don't you come back with me and have some? Then I'll try to clean those pants for you. I have some stain remover that does wonders with mud. I'll have them fixed up in a jiffy."

"Well, . . ." I hesitate, looking toward town. "I have some shopping to do," I say, even as a voice in my head tells me to go with Diana and enjoy the rare gift of some company. It's been so long since I've talked to anyone, and besides, I'm too wet to go anywhere now, so that's just an excuse. Even Diana, who doesn't know me well, must see that. She gently takes my arm and steers me to the car, guiding me the way she does with Sophia. There's something comforting about having someone tell me what to do, so meekly I go with her.

When we get to the house, I try not to look at the dolls that surround me. Keeping my eyes straight ahead, I follow Diana up to her room on the second floor, where she gives me a pair of sweat pants to wear.

"I'll put up the tea. Come on down when you're all set," she says, shutting the door.

Once she's gone, I look around her small room, which she obviously shares with Carlo. There are two twin beds jutting out from a bare wall. Each is covered with a pale pink spread and has pillows in faded floral cases. The bed closer to the door has a teddy bear lying facedown on it. The bear wears red pants with matching suspenders. I pick him up and turn him over, seeing the red bow tied around his neck. He's really adorable. There's also a jumble of other stuffed animals and toys piled on top of the headboard.

This colorful mess is in sharp contrast to the headboard of Diana's bed, which is nearer to the window and is empty except for a string of shiny black rosary beads. The round balls glint like onyx in the afternoon light streaming through the window. The sun turns them into dark fireballs and reminds me of when I was young and I used to have similar beads except mine were a lighter shade.

I would slide the glossy beads through my nervous fingers at night, never sure of what the motion would bring but knowing that I was reaching for something. Even though I wasn't raised all that religiously, my mother had insisted that I have something to believe in. My father disagreed with her philosophy but he gave in, not willing to fight against something she believed in so strongly.

When I became older and disillusioned because whatever intangible thing I had been waiting for never occurred, I gave up such traditional beliefs and stowed the beads deep in a box at the back of my closet. It fit in between my little bible and the silver cross on a thin chain my grandmother gave me when I turned eight but which I never wore. The idea of Jesus hanging on that cross, nails through his hands, sickened me in Sunday School when the teacher would talk about the crucifixion and I got stomach aches just picturing such cruelty.

Now, I am reminded of my uneasiness about the whole subject as my eyes move from Diana's beads to a thick wooden cross attached to her wall above them. It's nailed up unevenly, as though put up in a hurry. My mother has similar crosses placed around her house. My father seems to tolerate them pretty well but I simply can't bear to look at them. I avert my eyes from their glossy surfaces, pretending that I don't even notice their presence.

But in the bareness of Diana's half of the room, her religious symbols seem to take on new, weightier dimensions than my mother's do. While my mother's are interspersed with pictures of me as a child and of my aunts, uncles, and cousins, Diana's are the sole decoration on her side of the room. Yet I get the sense that Diana's religious beliefs take the place of any other attachments, except for Carlo, who must be the very center of what I suspect may be a lonely existence.

Even as I'm thinking this, I catch a glimpse of my face in a small mirror leaning on the dresser against the wall. I look tired and pale and jealous. I turn away from myself and stare down at the bed, shamefaced, because perhaps I'm trying to turn Diana's life into an empty book in order to rationalize the fact that she has a child while I have none. This pettiness floods me with shame and I try to push the whole subject away and concentrate on slipping into the sweats Diana has left me. When I'm dressed, I gather up my own ruined pants to bring to her down in the kitchen.

Diana has steaming mugs already placed on the table and a plate of fresh cookies. It's been a while since I've felt hungry like this.

"Mmmmm. Smells wonderful." I take a sip of my tea and reach for a cookie, watching as Diana brings my pants to the sink and treats the mud with a squirt of stain remover.

"I made them earlier today as a treat for Carlo. He's a good boy, putting up with this house and all the trouble that Sophia gives him."

"Yeah, it must be tough for a little boy to live here in the winter. There aren't many kids around here, are there?"

"A few, but he misses his friends. I can see it in his face. He doesn't fit in here. But soon we'll be going home."

"Home?"

"The Bronx. That's where we live during the winter. With my sister Amelia. I help her clean houses and she gives me a place to stay."

"Oh. I didn't realize that. How long have you been here on the island?"

"Since May. We were supposed to stay only till September, but then Sophia's daughter had to go away for a while, and she asked us to stay on a bit longer. I couldn't afford to turn her down. This is such a good job and I like getting Carlo out of the city for the hottest months. We've been coming here for the past three years."

"I've been coming here every summer since I was a very young child, just about Carlo's age. It's always been my favorite place. I am sure he's forming some wonderful memories, just like I did."

"There's lots of good here for him, but Sophia is quite a lot of work. She's driving us both crazy these days. I'll be glad to get back to New York. As Carlo gets older he needs more stability than this, but the money helps us a lot. Oh, well." She sighs and shakes her head, then asks me, "When do you think you'll be heading home? You said you live in Boston, right? That's such a nice city."

"Mmmmm." Home. The question makes me think again. Something I don't want to do.

"I don't know," I say, an emptiness opening up inside my chest. I want to go home, but I'm also afraid. There's a lot of pain that I left there, and I'm worried that it will be waiting to reattach itself to me when I return there.

"How is your husband doing? How could you bear to leave him for so long?" Diana asks, a shadow crossing her face. "I heard about your baby, you know, and I'm very, very sorry about it. It must be hard, but your husband must be your best friend, right? Shouldn't you be together now? Supporting each other through this? I just don't understand how you could come here without him."

Diana sounds so much like my friend Sonja. If she were here with me, I'm sure Sonja would say something similar. But how in the world can I begin to explain my actions to anyone, even myself, when my feelings are all so confused and jumbled together?

For a moment, I want to hurt Diana. "What about

Carlo's father? Why aren't you with him?" I feel bad when she winces.

"Carlo is illegitimate. I made a mistake when I was young. I was stupid then. I paid a high price for it, you know, having a baby on my own. I didn't want him, either."

"Didn't want who? The father or Carlo?" My question sounds too loud in the room.

"Carlo. I wasn't ready for a child. Not at all. I hated the idea, but I was raised to do my duty. I did what I had to, and I don't look back to regret it. My momma used to say 'What will be, will be' and I believe it."

"You didn't want that beautiful boy?" My stomach clenches at the thought.

Diana starts to cry silently. She sits still for a moment, letting the tears run down her cheeks, then excuses herself for a moment. When she returns, she's holding several old, crumbled photographs.

"This is Carlo when he was a baby," she says, pushing a picture before me. "Look at how sweet he was. Over time I grew to love him very much." Then she holds out another picture, this one of a man who has the same full lips and cheeks as Carlo. "This is him, Carlo's father. He was ten years older than me and I loved him very much, but he thought I was just a kid, someone to have fun with. It hurt a lot when he left."

"Does he know about Carlo?"

"Ay. I told him that last night, before he left me. He yelled at me, something about being stupid and careless. I was 17, on the pill, but I didn't understand about taking it every day. I thought it would be OK. He yelled at me, cursing in Spanish, and slapped me, hard, so the breath left my lungs and then he pushed me out of his way. I fell against the wall, holding my face, and I cried so hard and wished that the baby would disappear. But the man, his name was Luis, he disappeared instead. I never saw him again, but eight months later little Carlo came."

"I'm sorry."

"Please," Diana says, sniffing, wiping at her cheeks with her fists. "Don't be sorry. Since I heard about your baby, your daughter, I've been sick inside, feeling so guilty that I didn't even want a child and here it is, that I have one and yours is gone."

Her words cause something to dislodge inside me and my vision breaks. I feel like I might faint. I lean my head down against the tabletop, willing the awful rush of weakness that is moving through my body to go away. Then Diana is there, resting her cool hand against my hair, stroking my back, telling me everything will be OK.

I think about Jim, and how I would feel if he ever left me, and I know that Diana is lucky to have her young son. But she's right. I'm very lucky, too, to have Jim. Especially after all of the time I waited for him. I also know that I could easily have been in the same situation she's in.

Chapter 17

The more time I spend away from Jim, the more I find myself thinking about him. Talking with Diana has intensified this. Now, more than ever, his different faces are here, etched against the surface of the lighthouse. There are so many sides to him that I have grown to know so well over the years, pulling me tighter and tighter to him, wrapping me up in this feeling called love. There's the young Jim who wanted just to be friends, the older Jim who couldn't quite commit, the wonderful Jim who asked me to marry him. Then there's also the newer Jim who wasn't sure if he wanted children, the Jim who weighed Lily's pink dress in the palm of his hand, and the one who waited eagerly to hold Lily.

I'm sitting on the couch now, holding little Lily myself. My little princess. Her face glows like a moon in the circle of light from the lamp beside us. I stop in mid-thought and stroke her head, letting my fingers sink against the softness of her skin and her hair. It's almost 10 p.m. already, but she doesn't seem to want to sleep. (I'm tired, though. All these thoughts are draining.)

The little ghostly Lily reminds me of the current Jim, the one who waits now in the city for me, the one who has come out since the real Lily's death. This Jim is just a blending of all those other faces, a way to stitch all of his personalities together into one deeper, more complex, face. This face is the one I can't seem to escape. More and more I find that I'm missing Jim. In all our years together I've still never quite been able to define what it is exactly about him that I love so much, yet I keenly feel the absence of him now. He rests in my chest like a muscle strain. I savor the pain, even as I try to escape it.

Sometimes when I look in the mirror, I can see Jim there, see his reflection coming up behind me, feel his eyes pulling at me from different directions. This is a strange feeling and one I'm not comfortable with. I just feel so lost without that man, I try to find a glimpse of him in any way I can. Some nights in Ida's room, I imagine the bed is a raft cast adrift in the vastness of the blue ocean, surrounded by ripples of water and no slice of land. Other times I'm a weightless balloon lifting out of a child's hand, floating higher and higher on a curve of the wind, blowing out of sight. I know if Jim were here, he would rescue me by grabbing the string or helping me navigate. If I have these kinds of thoughts, what kinds of things could Jim be thinking of? And what is his life like without *me*?

The longer that time passes without a letter, the more I worry about him and find myself trying to capture him in my mind, wanting to find some kind of connection. I find myself trying to walk through his days, trying to find a thread to stitch the distance together.

What is he doing *right now*? *Right at this very moment*? Hmmmm. I cradle my head against the back of the couch and try to imagine the answer.

I imagine: Jim enters the apartment quietly. It's after 10 p.m. and he doesn't want to wake me up. Then it hits him, I'm not even there. I've been living in that darn lighthouse for over three weeks now, yet he still hasn't gotten used to the idea. By the time he does, I'll probably be home already, he figures. That can't happen too soon for him, either. He wishes I would return to him, to my place in the bed where I belong. That's what Jim would be thinking right now. I'm sure of it.

It's cold in the apartment and he turns up the heat and slips out of his stiff gray suit jacket, slinging it onto the kitchen chair. That would annoy me if I were home, so he does it deliberately, taking liberties now when there's no one to scold him. Everything is a trade-off in this world. He pads into the bedroom, thinking about this as he turns on the light, and about how he would gladly hang the jacket on the hard wooden hanger where it belongs in our large bedroom closet, if that would bring me home.

He slides into his sweats, the navy blue ones worn soft at the knees from so much wear, and slips into his wrinkled B.C. T-shirt. He can smell the fabric softener clinging to the cotton as he pulls it over his head. He's really not very hungry these days but he figures he should eat. His pants have been feeling loose around the waist this week. Whenever Jim and I try to diet together, he loses weight so much faster than I do. It just doesn't seem fair. Now, he's suddenly thin without even trying. He pours cereal into a bowl, listens to the crunch, wonders if he'll make the effort to really eat it. He picks the Frosted Flakes, my cereal, instead of his Corn Puffs. He reasons to himself that this is because my cereal will soon go stale.

He feels bone tired after working so late, and his shoulders ache from hunching over his desk studying briefs, trying to come up with an airtight case. He can feel the strain catching up to him now. He pinches the ache in the bridge of his nose with his fingers, feeling the pressure building there. He tries to will it away, make it disappear. Maybe unshed tears are forming there, but he likes to think it's something else, something like his cold coming back instead. That makes more sense to him. He's been working so hard he hasn't been able to completely shake the germs; he can still taste them in the back of his throat, that congested feeling that lingers there. His chest, too, feels tight and aching. He doesn't believe in loneliness so he has to find some rational reason for these things.

But he can't help wondering if the vague aches and pains he feels could be soothed away by the touch of my hand if only I were sitting there on the couch beside him. I usually sit on the side of the couch closest to the television set. He imagines he can see my indentation etched in the couch cushions there. He feels my leg brushing against his, remembers how solid and warm it feels. If I were there now he bets there would be a lightness flowing through him, starting in his stomach and stretching up, making him weightless and free like a feather. But he's alone. Heavy and slow and alone in the living room, sitting in the dark, with only the glow from the television over there and the moon through the window. The room has a dark purple cast to it with deeper pockets of shadows.

He thinks about what his life would be like now if Lily had lived. She would be asleep in the next room and we would listen to her steady breathing over the monitor we had hooked up the week before she was born. There are two speakers: one in the bedroom and one in the living room. The speakers would carry her soft little breaths into the room, magnifying the sound until it became a loud throb. He feels his pulse quicken with the imagined rhythm, swelling toward the center of its beat. He pretends that I'm leaning my head on his shoulder, resting my hand against his leg. The thought makes him feel better. It makes him feel like he's giving me something, even if it's just a place to prop my head.

But he knows in truth that he can't even give me that now, and this knowledge, more than anything else, makes him feel that he has failed me. I'm off in that old lighthouse, even though he didn't want me to go. The reality is that I'm not here, and neither is Lily, and he hates the fact that he has no control of the situation. He shakes off the thought, like a dog shakes rain, freeing it from the hairs of its coat. He wants to throw off his reality from his skin, his blood, his arms and legs, his brain. He wishes he could be free of it all, but no matter how hard he tries, all these things follow him, making him feel old and beaten and empty.

He goes into our room, his body a sharp angle as he leans to switch off the lamp by the bed and then stretches out on the mattress, trying to ignore the sound vibrating through him, a deepening chord that fills him like a violin string gently being plucked. This sound is the pain that he lives with every day. He can't capture this pain and translate it into words and images, like I'm able to do with my pain, but he feels it nonetheless, letting it crest like a building wave. It's like a whole ocean lives on inside of him.

Poor Jim. I can see this scene so sharply in my mind even though he's so far away and really it's my Lily here, Lily lying beside me, but she's fading into the distance and Jim is the dominant one, looming bright with his imaginary presence. I hold Lily in my arms like a basket, the two of us resting alone on the couch. No matter which way I turn, though, I think of Jim.

I want to get him out of my mind so I switch off the lamp, encasing the room in the dark blanket of night. But he refuses to go away. His pain is here, trapped in the blackness. I feel it being carried on the endless waves that hit the rocks and echo right into the room. I imagine the sound is Jim, calling out to me. *Claire*, I imagine he calls. *Claire. Please come home. Please, honey, come back to me.*

Chapter 18

I got another letter from my mom this week, asking me to come home. Thanksgiving is in a few days and she said she wants me there to celebrate the day with her and Dad, and Jim. But how in the world can I sit there in her steamy kitchen, eating turkey and stuffing and cranberry sauce, and thanking God for all our blessings?

In her letter, my mother said that she understands the pain I'm in, but feels it important that I realize what I *do* have rather than just focusing on the negative. I think she's afraid that if I don't thank God for my family and my husband and my health, then something else bad might happen to one of them or to me, and I'll be even worse off than I am now. Sometimes thinking about my mother simply tires me out. I can't imagine having to go through life the way she does.

On the other hand, in some ways maybe she's right and I really should appreciate what I have, because I know now first-hand how quickly it can be taken away. What if my marriage evaporates with the speed and thoroughness that Lily disappeared from my life? I do love Jim very much, despite our differences, and I don't want to be cavalier and take our relationship for granted. While I had the strength and the patience to wait for him in the past, I'm not completely sure that he can do the same thing for me. I think men thrive in the warmth of a woman's love and without it, they wither. If Jim withers too much, he may just give up on me completely. Part of my fear probably stems from all of the effort that I put into making our relationship work. Even though Jim can't quite pinpoint exactly what it is that made him marry me, I think that it was because I was so nice to him, and so persistent, that eventually he realized his life was empty without me in it.

Now, though, some of my niceness has died with Lily, and I'm just struggling to survive in her absence. I don't have the strength or the will to coddle him anymore and deal with his moods, trying to pull the "real" Jim out of the black hole of his silence. For the first time in our relationship, I'm focusing all my attention on me, and on Lily's ghost. Like it or not, he'll have to fend for himself.

Since Jim hasn't written to me in over a week, I guess that means he's not liking this new side of me very much. I wrote him a note this morning, telling him that although I haven't seen him in almost three weeks, I really do miss him a lot. In fact, I just can't seem to get him out of my mind. I also wrote a letter to my mother, explaining why I won't be coming home for her dinner on Thursday. Just thinking about the Thanksgiving feast my mom prepares every year makes me feel rather sick. Maybe I'll have my own Thanksgiving dinner here in the lighthouse, for me and for Lily. I should probably at least thank God for sending Lily's spirit to me. For that I truly am grateful.

Lily is sleeping in the basket right now, resting on her stomach with her hands balled into tiny fists. I love the way she sticks her bottom up in the air when she sleeps, occasionally whimpering when she moves. I wonder if ghosts dream at all.

A knock at the door startles me. I turn away from the baby, curious to know who could be there.

"It's me, Diana, and Carlo."

At Diana's cheery voice, I swing the door open eagerly.

I'm glad to see her, and her son, but at the same time, I find myself regretting their intrusion into my precious time with Lily.

"Come on in."

"Thanks," Diana says, "but we can't stay. We just wanted to say goodbye and drop off some brownies. Carlo and I made them last night. We're finally going home, to New York. It's long overdue."

My stomach shifts at this news. Despite the short time I've spent with Diana, I realize I'll really miss her.

"I helped mama make the brownies for you," Carlo chimes in. "I tried one, too. They're yummy!"

"Will you be coming back at all?" I ask.

"Not this year," Diana says. "This is it for us. Will you be leaving soon, too?"

"I don't know," I say, shaking my head. "My plans are rather up in the air."

Diana looks at me hesitantly. "Will you be all right here alone? Don't you think it might be time to go home? Go back to your husband now? I don't mean to butt in, but I'm sure he needs you at this time, and you need him. Please forgive me for speaking my mind, but I'm worried about you staying here. I'm quite sure all of this solitude isn't good for you in this state of mind. How could it be?"

"I appreciate your concern," I tell her. "It's nice of you to care, but really, I'm fine." I'm not angry with Diana for being so honest with me. In fact, her words bring tears to my eyes, because a part of me longs to get onto the next ferry and go home. But I know that I can't. Not at this time.

From across the room, Lily softly begins to cry.

Carlo hears the sound and wanders into the living room, his eyes lighting up as he sees Lily.

"Look, Mama." He points to the baby. "Look at how cute. I didn't know you had a baby here! I thought she was with all of the angels and God."

"Carlo," Diana scolds. "What are you talking about? There's no baby here." She grabs Carlo's arm and ushers him back toward the door. "I'm so sorry, Claire. How awful. He must have heard me talking on the phone with my sister about your situation. I hope you don't mind my sharing this with her. I guess Carlo overheard and somehow the idea of a baby must have stuck in his mind."

I smile at her and at Carlo, glad that his vision is as sharp as mine.

"Come on now, Carlo. We've got to go. Sophia is waiting in the car, remember?" She glances at her watch, then turns to me. "Our ferry leaves soon and we don't want to miss it. We're meeting Sophia's daughter on the mainland. She's taking Sophia to an assisted living home. Her daughter thinks she shouldn't be on her own anymore. She's been having more and more trouble staying 'with it' lately."

"I just wanted to see the baby," Carlo says, kicking his toe against the hard floor. "I can hear her crying."

"Shhhh," Diana scolds. "I really am so sorry," she says. "He must hear the wind and be confused. Children get all sorts of strange things in their minds."

Diana hustles Carlo back onto the porch, even as the little boy tries to resist her touch, squirming to get another glimpse of Lily. Diana firmly holds him with one arm, reaching with the other to give me a big hug. Despite her wiry build, I can feel her strength and determination in the motion. Then she releases me abruptly and starts to walk away, but pauses, looking over her shoulder at me, as if there's something she needs to say.

"Claire, I'm just so worried about you. Being here alone isn't right. Please, go home. Really. Please, Claire. I know it's none of my business, but—"

I bite my lip.

"I'll think about it." That's all I can promise her now, as she turns away and leads Carlo down the beach to where the taxi waits. I stand in the doorway and watch the vehicle pull away. It's getting foggy out, and almost instantly, the white car turns in the heaviness of the ocean mist, disappearing from sight.

I go back inside and feel more alone than I have in a while. Even Lily's presence doesn't seem to make me feel better. Perhaps I need a brisk walk to clear my head. I decide we should go to the post office, so I can mail Jim's and my mother's letters. With Diana gone, suddenly I'm longing for the easy flow of adult conversation.

Jim and I have always talked very well, and sometimes we would lie in bed at night debating different issues until the early hours of the morning. While I haven't thought about that in a while, now I find that I miss it all at once.

Outside, the fog is growing worse and even my layers of clothing can't hide the deepening chill. There's that extra bite to the air that signals winter is fast approaching. I've forgotten my gloves and I hesitate for a minute on the lighthouse bridge, wondering whether I should go back and get them. But I'm too lazy to turn around and unlock the door, so I just keep on going, blowing on my fingertips to warm them and shaking them occasionally to try to keep them from getting numb.

I stroll down the small stretch of the beach and then toward the road. I have Lily slung in a huge straw bag I found in Ida's hall closet. I covered her with the white blanket, tucking it tightly to hold in her warmth. The bag's handle straps rest over my arm, and the straw pouch sways when I walk, almost like a rocking chair or a cradle.

The fog hangs over the air like smoke, and it turns the road and grass and the houses I pass as I continue forward into faint gray outlines. I feel like I'm breast-stroking through the thickness of the cold sky, pushing back layers of clouds as I move, trying to surface for air, like dreaming.

It takes about 10 or 15 minutes to get to Main Street, which is pretty quiet at this time of year. In the summer, tourists fill the sidewalk with their energy and noise and excitement to be here. All the shops are open, displaying beautiful ceramics and handcrafted gifts. In winter, though, most people are gone and many of the stores are closed and there's a hush that falls over the town like the quiet you find beneath the dome of an umbrella.

The post office isn't that much farther, just around the corner and down the side street a block, but I'm chilled and a little out of breath when I get there. A small table has been set up just inside with complimentary coffee and hot chocolate on it. This is one of the things I really like about the island. A genuine warmth and hospitality that flows from the residents here that's missing in the anonymity of the city. I can't imagine the post office near my apartment in Boston ever offering its customers anything to eat or drink.

I take a Styrofoam cup in my freezing hands and fill it with a packet of hot chocolate and steaming water. The powder evaporates and turns the liquid into pools of chocolate. There's also a basket of stirrers there and I take one, using the plastic stick to mix the liquid and powder until they're perfectly blended.

A little girl in a pink quilted parka stands in line with her mother a few feet away, over by the postal windows. She watches me closely as I take a sip of the steaming drink, letting the warmth flow through me. She's a pretty child, with big brown eyes and curly dark hair that she wears in two pigtails. She reminds me of a darker version of what Lily might have been. As her mom turns to talk to the postal worker, the girl edges away from her, moving toward me. While Carlo's solid male presence didn't seem to threaten Lily, next to the vibrant little girl I can feel Lily's strength fading away.

"Hi," I say, smiling at the little girl, who comes right up to me and rests her head against my leg.

"What's your name?" I ask her.

"Elizabeth," she says, reaching her hand up toward mine.

"I like the name Elizabeth," I say, taking the hand and marveling at the warmth that flows from her to me. "I'm Claire." Touching her hand is nothing like touching Lily. Even though Lily is my own daughter, there's a feel to a real hand that a ghost or a spirit can't possibly achieve. So even as I tell Elizabeth my name, I'm overcome with a deep rush of sorrow.

There's a rosy glow to Elizabeth's cheeks and an excitement that flows through her as she tells me about her father and her ballet lessons and kindergarten, until her mother is done and turns to reclaim her. Then her mother smiles at me and Elizabeth waves goodbye and scurries off to go home. My eyes hungrily watch her go, her small form graceful in its movements. She skips as she walks, trying to keep up with her mother. My heart aches at the sight.

After she's gone, I peek into my bag to check on Lily, and I'm not at all surprised to see that she's gone. She couldn't compete with Elizabeth's liveliness. Then it's my turn in line and, still feeling sad, I ask the postal clerk for a book of stamps. She's the same woman who's behind the counter every time I come, and she smiles at me as if she remembers who I am.

"How are you liking the lighthouse?" she asks today, and I'm surprised for a moment, then remember what a small town this island is and how everyone knows everyone else's business around here.

"I like it a lot," I say, fumbling in my wallet for my money.

"Been scary for you, what with those old stories about the ghosts and all?" she asks, sliding the stamps across the counter with her thumbs. "I hope no one's been trying to spook you about that," she adds, counting out the wad of bills I've handed her.

I stiffen for a moment, afraid that she knows about Lily's ghost. Is that why she said such a thing? But then I remember hearing different rumors and tall tales about ghosts over the years I've spent on this island. I haven't thought about those old stories in a long time.

"What's the real story about the ghosts?" I ask cautiously, feeling curious now about what others have seen in the lighthouse.

"There are lots of different tales about them," she says. "Of course, I don't believe in them myself, but some people here take the ghosts very seriously. Over the years, different lighthouse keepers have seen and heard different things that they couldn't explain, or else didn't want to. Things like a white haze floating through the rooms, strange sounds in the night, a soft breeze rushing through the house, the sound of footsteps when they were sure no one was there. I think it's the way the lighthouse is perched on the rocks. It catches the wind in its walls and vibrates with the swell of the waves, and some people would rather think that these things are a ghost. It makes them feel important.

"But the most popular story is from about 30 years ago. A young girl of about seven or eight drowned on that beach. For the next few years, her mother would walk up and down the shore searching for her, hoping that her daughter would somehow come back to her. The woman plumb lost her mind, you know, over that death. Her only child, too, so she felt it even more keenly than if she had another child to help fill up some of that gaping space in her heart. So every night, even in the rain, the woman was out there, pacing the shoreline. She insisted that her daughter did come back, or her ghost did, anyway, and they would walk along the sand together. It was so sad. The mother thought that the little ghost slept in the lighthouse at night, and some summer nights she slept on the lighthouse bridge, wanting to be close to her child. She thought the daughter would be afraid of the dark if she wasn't close by."

"What a shame," I say, my heart going out to that poor mother. I can relate to her pain more than I want to. I thank the postal clerk for sharing these interesting stories and, feeling strangely pensive, I go into the lobby to check my postal box. I fit my key into the hole and listen to the lock slide open, then feel the door lift. I bend down to peer into the darkness of the box. There's a single letter perched inside, resting against the metal cubbyhole wall. It's addressed to me in Jim's writing and I feel a burst of relief to finally hear from him. But that relief drowns, seconds later, when I read the words he has written.

He tells me that he's fine but my mother is sick. She suffered a minor stroke and although she's out of danger, he thinks I should come home. I realize it must have happened right after she sent the last letter about Thanksgiving. Jim says he wishes he could have called to tell me the news, but since I had Ida's phone turned off while I'm here—I didn't want anyone to be able to reach me—he had to inform me by mail. He also says that he thought of sending a telegram, but didn't want to alarm me in my 'precarious' state, whatever that means, and he thought a letter would be better. Standing there in the empty post office lobby with his letter in my hand, I bury my face in my arm and start to cry.

Chapter 19

My flight back to Boston is uneventful.

After regaining my composure, I called Jim at work from the phone in the drug store near the post office. He said he would pick me up at the airport and take me to the hospital this evening to see my mom. She's at the same hospital where Lily was born. Jim assured me that my mother will be fine. She just needs to stay in the hospital for a few days for observation. Already she's recovered her speech, and the side of her face that Jim said was paralyzed at first has gone back to almost normal. Despite these reassurances, I know I won't be able to rest easy till I see her.

Since Lily's ghost had disappeared, I obviously couldn't take her with me, but I think that's for the best. Lily belongs in the isolation and beauty of the island, not in the hustle and bustle and dirt of the city. I know she'll be fine until I get back, which hopefully won't be too long.

Besides, I have other things to worry about now.

I press my forehead against the cold glass of the airplane window, watching the tiny city spread out far below and twinkling. The sight reminds me of the miniature Christmas village my mother sets up on her side table in the living room each year, alongside the tree. I used to love fingering the small wooden buildings that are carved with exquisite detail. Then the city begins to grow larger as we near the airport. The plane is really small—it seats only eight—but I'm the only person onboard except for the pilot. I can see the series of bright lights on the control board from my seat behind him. It's just starting to get dark out, and as we begin to descend, the plane flies through the mist of a cloud, and for a few seconds my view is obliterated as we become surrounded by the whiteness. I feel bathed in the softness of the color and consistency, which looks like handfuls of cotton that have been stretched really thin. The whiteness reminds me of Lily. And of cotton candy.

When I was young, my mother would let me eat a stick of that sticky pink sugary stuff when we went to a carnival or an amusement park, but only if I promised to brush my teeth extra well afterward. She always kept a toothbrush and small tube of toothpaste for me in a sandwich bag stuck away in her purse. She would make me brush my teeth in the bathroom. I used to hate standing there in a public place, spitting out the toothpaste bubbles into the sink, but I have to admit that this diligence paid off: To this day I've never had a cavity.

Thinking about this now, and remembering those outings with my mother, I can't wait to see her again and make sure she's all right.

The plane lands smoothly and I hurry into the terminal building, my eyes on the lookout for Jim. He's standing there, by the security gate, waiting for me. He looks exactly the same as he did when I left him: tall, strong, solid.

"Oh, Jim," I say as I rush toward him, my eyes filling with water. God, how I've missed him. Even through my worry about my mom, the full weight of our separation hits me, even more strongly now that he's right here in front of me than it ever did when we were miles apart.

"I'm glad you're back," he says.

A face up close has so many more layers and nuances

than when you simply recall it in your mind. Gratefully, I reach up and run my fingers over his rough skin, feeling the curve of his cheeks and his chin, the way I imagine a blind person 'sees' what someone looks like.

"I missed you so much," I whisper, my pulse quickening as I trace his face, drawing it to life, probing every inch of it as though I'm going to be quizzed. I can smell his familiar scent and I breathe in deeply to hold it inside me. This is the man I've woken up next to almost every morning for the past four years, glued up against his skin, the strong knock of his heartbeats against his chest. This is also the father of my child.

Flickers of Lily dance across his face and this makes me think of her now, and I wonder how she's doing alone. I'm so worried about her and about my mom. But at least Jim is here with me now. In some ways, that has to be enough. I let the sight and touch and smell of him press in on me and obliterate everything else for a moment.

Jim stands still under my scrutiny for as long as he can, probably sensing the turmoil running through me. Finally, as if he can bear it no more, he takes my hand in his, the heat flowing between us like an electric current. Then he leans over to kiss me. The dry coolness of his lips lingers against mine and there's the curve of his body against my stomach and hip. I memorize the shape and feel of him again. People rush by us, coming and going places, weighted down by luggage and children and noise, but they melt in a blur, just dashes of color, no real shapes. Jim is the only shape I can see. There's the rough prickle of his short hair beneath my fingers and I tug at the strands, wanting to pull him even closer to me.

Then I stretch up to burrow my nose against his neck like a squirrel, inhaling his scent, and I wrap my arms around him tightly, luxuriating in the weight of him. Jim hugs me back so hard I'm almost suffocating, but I don't even mind. I feel safer than I have in a long, long time. For a few moments, it feels like life before Lily.

But on the car ride to the hospital, this safety is threatened again when I remember. The memory comes on me like a flu does, creeping up so quickly you don't notice it until suddenly, surprisingly, you realize you feel horrible. I sit there, anxious, feeling a chasm separating us again as it had before I left. I'm thinking of the awful ride home from the hospital with Jim last month, and I wonder if he's remembering the same thing.

Several floors above in the maternity ward, my mother's room at the hospital looks similar to the way mine did. When Jim and I get there, at first I feel shy. The hospital corridors seem to dwarf me and I hate the antiseptic smell that tries to hide traces of illness but doesn't quite succeed.

I linger in the doorway to mom's room. She looks so small in the sterile bed. There are silver rails like a makeshift crib for adults and I think, fleetingly, of the bed rails I had as a young child to keep me from falling off the mattress during the night.

Jim goes over to the bed and I slowly follow, noticing how dry and lined my mother's pale skin seems against the whiteness of her pillowcase. Her eyes are closed and her eyelids are almost translucent. The foreign sight fills me with ice. There are tubes going into her arm and a tube for oxygen in her nose; a monitor next to the bed follows her heartbeat, sort of like the one in the delivery room that I'd been hooked up to.

We tiptoe over near the bed, not wanting to disturb her, and it's as if she senses our presence. Her eyes slowly open, and her face lights up and she smiles. The smile seems to bring her back to life. Her skin smoothes out and softens right away and she regains some color and vitality. It's amazing to see the change.

"My Claire," she says, reaching her arms out to hug me, mindless of the tubes. "Come here and let me see you again."

Carefully, I step around wires and lean into her embrace. I'm surprised by the strength of her grasp. It's as if my presence has given new hope to my mother. When my father comes later, he agrees with me; my being here has really helped my mother a lot. Remembering my mother's beliefs, I say a quick, silent prayer to God, thanking him. I can't take any chances.

The air is dry in the room and I feel really thirsty. I'm suddenly craving an ice-cold diet Coke. I leave Jim and my father talking to my mom, and I go to find a soda machine. There doesn't seem to be one on this floor, and almost without thought, I get onto the elevator and find myself pressing the button for the maternity ward.

Seconds later, the doors blink open. Hesitantly, I step out. I remember so clearly the day the nurse guided me here in a wheelchair. I remember the contractions and the pain and the excitement I felt then, anticipating Lily.

I step slowly down the pale sterile hallway, averting my eyes from the open doors of the rooms. I don't want to see a new mother breastfeeding her infant or, worse yet, someone cuddling with her husband and baby on the bed. I look straight ahead until I come to the nursery where the brand-new babies are. There's a glass wall separating them from the rest of the world, sort of like the tank my class had for our bunny rabbit when I was in elementary school. But the nursery has a ceiling instead of the tank's top, and the way to enter is through the door, which is closed and restricted to keep uninvited visitors from entering.

Through the transparent wall, I eye the rows of tiny, red-faced babies peering up from the bassinets. Tentatively,

I rub my fingers against the glass, leaving my fingerprints. All the babies look the same in their tiny gowns, each with a minuscule hospital bracelet on his or her wrist, announcing their identities to the world. Lily's ghost was so still and white, such a contrast to these red, vivacious babies. They squirm in their spots as they get used to the place they've entered.

Standing there, I start to cry, silently, my shoulders trembling from the effort. I'm crying for myself, but also for Lily and Jim and my parents. I'm crying for all of us. A nurse passes me standing there and she looks like she's going to stop and speak to me for a minute, but then she catches sight of my tears and veers away, leaving me alone there with the infants and my pain.

I'm still crying inside when Jim and I get home from the hospital around 9 p.m., after visiting hours have ended. There's no outward trace of my tears, though. I have enough makeup under my eyes to hide the telltale smudges.

Jim and I sit on the couch, trying to get used to each other again. Even through all the times I've been thinking about him, I haven't tried to imagine what it would be like to be together again. Now that I'm here, there's an awkwardness I couldn't have predicted. Jim turns on the television set and we sit in silence. An *I Love Lucy* rerun is on, and we watch as Lucy and Ethel concoct one of their infamous schemes. It's so much easier to relax into their made-up lives than to try to pick up where mine has ended.

"Do you want to watch this?" Jim asks, holding the remote control in his hand.

"Sure." There are so many things I want to say to Jim, to tell him about my time in the lighthouse. I want to describe to him how the beach looks in winter and I want to tell him about Lily's ghost and how I've become a mother again. I also want to tell him about Ida's beautiful love letters. And about the sad story the clerk at the post office told me about the woman whose daughter drowned. But I don't know how to bring all of this up. There seems to be a stiltedness that separates us now and has nothing to do with distance. All of this time I've been waiting to be with Jim and I had thought that being in the same room was all it would take for us to reconnect. Now, I realize how wrong I was to assume that. We're still miles apart even though only two inches separates our legs.

I'm getting sleepy and I lean back on the couch, closing my eyes and letting my head drift toward Jim. When my cheek rests against his shoulder, a wave of tenderness grows in my stomach. Maybe we'll be able to work this out, I think, getting used to the soft curve of his arm. But then Jim abruptly jerks his body away—on purpose or a reflex, I'm not sure which. Then he gets up and goes into the bedroom. A few minutes later I hear the hard rush of the shower hitting against the tile tub.

I'm unsure if Jim is angry with me for having gone away or if his coldness now is because my presence reminds him of Lily.

Lily. What would it be like if she were here? I wonder what her nursery looks like now. I decide to be brave and check while Jim is in the bathroom. Quietly, I get up and go to the closed door of the room, curious to see what's left inside. I had been afraid to open the door when I first came back from the hospital all those weeks ago, but now I'm dying to see that special room again. The rest of the apartment is empty of any reminders of Lily's existence but maybe Jim has kept some things shut away in here for us to reminisce over later, when we can stand it.

I slowly open the door to the room, wincing as it creaks on its hinges. When the noise stops, I step inside. It's very dark so I flick on the light, flooding the room in brightness.

There are no baby things here. That much is clear. Jim has gotten rid of everything, exactly the way I had asked him to, and converted the room back into a generic den. But instead of feeling glad he did, I'm filled with a deep, empty sorrow. My eyes wash over the couch, the end table, the magazine rack. All solid, familiar things that make my stomach clench and leave me feeling hollow. There's no crib and no mobile. No sign of any of the tiny baby clothes or pastel furry animals or plastic blocks we had picked out over the past few months, getting ready to welcome Lily.

I sit down weakly on the old convertible couch, feeling the cushions sink under my weight and wishing there was some small memory to grasp onto here. Not a memory of the pain that accompanied Lily's death, but a memory of the pleasure with which we had awaited her.

I finger the soft fabric of a velvety blanket thrown over the couch arm and think about Lily's ghost, who waits for me in the lighthouse. Soon I must return to her.

This thought is on my mind when I climb into bed beside Jim sometime later. It's funny how the whole time I was in the lighthouse, I had longed to be back beside Jim in our bed and now that I'm here, I just want to go back to the lighthouse and to Lily.

Jim rests his arm against mine as he sleeps but it still feels strange being with him again. In the nighttime, our legs tangle together but he's careful to avoid anything more, anything that could lead to sex. After the birth, the doctor told us we had to wait a while before being physically intimate again. I don't mind. I feel like Jim and I need to find our closeness in other ways, first.

In the morning, Jim and I dress in silence. Today is Thanksgiving and we're going to spend the day in the hospital with my parents. I slip into my red dress and Jim helps me with the zipper. Then I help him by ironing his white shirt. We are courteous to each other, but we tread carefully, sort of like formal guests rather than husband and wife or best friends.

My father has tried to make the hospital room look cheery with a big green plant by the bed and a tray with mashed potatoes and stuffing and a turkey breast set out for us. My mother has to eat the blander hospital food but she says the smell of our hot meal brings her appetite back and makes her eager to bite into the meager spread of tasteless food set out on the plate the nurse brought her.

Before we're allowed to eat, though, Mom makes us listen to her Thanksgiving prayer.

She thanks God for having us all here in her room and for helping her survive the stroke without too many complications. She also thanks him for bringing me here to celebrate this holiday together.

I find that I can honestly thank God, too. I thank him for my mother's recovery. Tomorrow she'll be going home and I, too, need to go home, to the lighthouse.

I suppose that Jim and I have been getting along all right, considering what we've been through this past month or two, but I'm also scared because I think there's something missing. It's as if the wonderful passion and color we shared has drained from our lives and now we go on with things like two people sleepwalking in black and white, talking and touching like normal but, at least on my part, not really feeling anything. I can't tell if Jim is angry at me for leaving him for those few weeks, or if the strain between us is still a remnant of Lily's death. He treats me like I'm someone with whom he's not really comfortable. Or as though I'm convalescing from a long illness. I hate all of this tiptoeing around and want to break through the barrier, yet I don't quite know how.

Before I leave Boston for the lighthouse again, I ask Jim to drive me to the cemetery so I can put flowers on Lily's grave. This is my first time back since the funeral and I have to brace myself for the onslaught of memories I know will follow. We bring tiny pink roses with us and Jim grimly parks the car at the edge of the park. The dried winter grass, punctuated by smooth gray slabs of stone, looks uncomfortably unfamiliar, and I try to keep my eyes blurred, careful not to focus on anything. We steadily cross the grass to Lily's grave without speaking or looking at each other.

When we arrive, I gently spread the roses across the tiny raised plot of land. There are other flowers already there, probably left by Jim and my parents. The petals have wilted in the cold but the sight of the stems fills me with sadness and I reach to Jim to hug him. He seems so sad and alone, like a lost child. He slowly reaches down and lifts a dried petal in his hands. Then he kneels to the ground and fingers the fragile piece as if it were a worry stone, rubbing it again and again until the petal crumbles into particles fine as dust. They trickle down like a soft rain shower, blending into the dirt so fine you can barely see them.

Then Jim starts to cry. His whole face breaks with the effort and he sits down on the ground, his body shaking. This sight shocks me and I stand there, watching him, frozen for a moment. I sit down beside him on the cold dirt and clasp him in my arms, crying. Our sobs blend together into one sound that seems to echo in the air.

Chapter 20

I return to the lighthouse eagerly. There's a layer of quiet that surrounds the beach and comforts me after the noise and pulse and brightness of the city. I'm walking along the bridge to the front door outlined in green, and already from here I can see Lily. She hovers in the window, watching me. She's like a white cloud framed against the glass, captured there, just a blur of misty shadow. My hands tremble and my heart pounds at the sight. I'm so very glad that she has come back to me.

The whole time while Jim and I were visiting Lily's grave, I couldn't stop thinking about her and wanting to see her. I'm sad that Jim is in so much pain, but I'm relieved, too, that he was finally able to release a tiny bit of it. I think that crying is the first step in healing for him. For me, though, my pain is of a different nature and crying a river wouldn't begin to soothe it. I search for answers in ways that can help me ease my way back to the life I'd been living before. But then again, maybe moving on is not the answer. My trip to the city confused me in a lot of ways. It was so wonderful to see Jim and yet, I also worry about the strain between us. How in the world will we ever move beyond a time in our lives that has been so terrible? I know that many couples eventually get divorced after they lose a child. I would never want that to happen to us, but am not quite sure how to avoid the danger.

These thoughts crowd my mind when as I enter the lighthouse, but the sight of Lily before me, hanging in the air like a fragile white flower waiting to be picked, distracts me. I run and scoop her into my arms, holding her tightly to me, breathing in the musty scent of the room that mingles with her lightness. Now that I'm here again, I realize how much I've missed everything.

I turn on the light and then walk around touching things, picking up a cushion here, moving a basket there, enjoying the way the surfaces feel beneath my fingertips. This helps to put me at ease in this place, which is unfamiliar again, even though I was gone for only a few days and still remember everything. Lily is slung on my hip the whole while, since I can't bear to put her down for even a second. Occasionally I lean in and kiss her fair head, loving the feeling of being a mother again.

Finally, when my arm tires and my back starts to ache, I put Lily down to sleep in the basket. Then I sit on the couch and watch her, unable to take my eyes off the whiteness of her skin and the pretty shape of her face. Softly I begin to sing, sweet lullabies that remind me of my childhood. The notes of the melodies gather and lift, floating up in the room the way feathers swirl in the wind, graceful in their ascent. They rise and dip and rise again, trailing into the air and blending into the whisper of the wind and the rolling surf. These sounds penetrate the walls of the house and seep into the small room, creating an impromptu orchestra.

Lily remains still and distant in the basket, not stirring at all as she sleeps. I keep pressing my hands against her small chest, which through the blanket feels soft and fragile. I wish I could freeze this time and savor the delicate details forever.

I doze off myself until loud, crashing noises startle me to life again. It takes me a minute to get my bearings, then I anxiously look to Lily, to be sure she is OK. She seems to be sleeping on, unaffected by the sound, safe in her cocoon. Then I go to the window and peer out into the early night, marveling at all the blackness that surrounds the lighthouse.

There seems to be no moonlight, just the glow from the lighthouse tower, which fills the beach with eerie shadows. Squinting into the night, I see that the stretch of sand, which usually lies flat and even on the ground, rises in the wind in angry sprays, some of them pelting the lighthouse with faint thumps. But this isn't the noise that woke me. It's the harsh pounding of the waves against the base of the tower that sounds loud and dangerous, like wood splitting open. I haven't heard this sound before and I don't know what to make of it. There must be quite a storm brewing.

Shivering at the thought, I check all of the windows to be sure they're securely fastened. Even though there doesn't seem to be a crack of space anywhere, it feels as if slivers of wind are slipping in somewhere, somehow. Then it starts to rain, heavy beats that tap and vibrate against the walls of the house, big, loud, and ominous.

Ida doesn't have a television—she says she doesn't like modern shows—but the radio in the kitchen is my landline to civilization. I turn it on, wanting to hear the weather forecast. The radio announcer's voice fills the room as though he's right here with me and my sleeping daughter, speaking to us.

"A Nor'easter is making its way through the east coast tonight, bringing with it bouts of heavy rain and wind, some gusts expected to reach up to 80 miles an hour. Flood warnings are in effect for Nantucket and parts of the Cape Cod shore. Residents who live near the beach are advised to close their homes and go to the emergency shelters that are being set up in the schools."

This news alarms me. My hands shake as I switch the radio off and go to get a sweater. I feel so cold in here and the rain seems like it's getting worse, drumming insistently on the roof, almost like someone is knocking. I have no car and it's too cold and wet and windy to walk to town in a storm. I would never make it. I grow more and more scared and I wish that Jim were here with me. He'd know what to do. The lighthouse sits so close to the ocean that I'm afraid it could be devastated by the storm, pulled right out and swallowed up by the raging ocean. Even with all its weight and bulk, there's a delicacy to the light tower and connecting house that makes me wonder how resilient they really are.

I try to push such thoughts away as I sit here, flipping through the pages of a magazine, occasionally glancing at Lily's sleeping form. Then the electricity goes out. The brightness of the room turns heavy with darkness and Lily disappears into the shroud of the blackness.

Ida has left candles on the windowsills, ready and waiting for this event. I find them by feeling my way through the obstacles in the room. It's hard to light a match in the dark, and it's not until a flash of lightning streaks the sky that I'm able to get the flame to catch. By candlelight, the room has new shadows and nuances. It's funny how the darkness sometimes reveals things that brightness obscures. Seeing Ida's objects now in a new way makes me think about my own items back in my apartment in Boston and I realize that I miss them more after my brief journey home.

My living room is much larger and more spacious than Ida's, with a smoothness to the soft lines of the furniture that seems to be missing here. I decorated in whites and creams and beiges, trying to capture the depth of the sand on a summer's day and give a soft, pleasing backdrop for my collection of unusual artwork. In contrast, Ida's main room is filled with dark wood and more colorful and lively fabrics, portraying more jumble and bustle than I feel comfortable with.

For the first time since I arrived several weeks ago, I feel almost claustrophobic in the lighthouse. This thought takes my mind off the storm for a few minutes, but the waves breaking against the building are always in the background, punctuating everything.

In a few minutes, a strange thing happens: some of the lights go back on but not in their full intensity. They seem weak and dim and I blink a few times, wondering if my eyes are failing me. It takes me a second before I remember there's a generator that powers the light tower and also serves as a backup for the electricity in the house. But the lights on so low are almost as eerie as having no light. I find a candle holder and rest the candle on the tabletop so I can try to read some more, but my hands are shaking so badly that I can't hold the magazine still and the candle casts shadows that make the words blur together. Finally, I put the magazine down and lean my head against the back of the couch, letting my thoughts flicker down to nothing.

Sometime during the night, I wake to the feel of the lighthouse rocking. I wonder if I would be safer outside than here, where I worry that the walls could come crashing down around me. It feels like the shape of the house is being stretched with each huff and puff of the wind, the way the Big Bad Wolf threatens to blow down the house in *The Three Little Pigs*. My mother used to read that story to me when I was a child, and I would giggle and clap my hands in delight at the thought. Now, though, the concept in real life is far from funny. I scoop Lily out of the basket and rock her against my chest, holding her there, wanting to keep both of us safe and sound and wondering how best to do this.

The front door, which I must have forgotten to lock, strangely swooshes open in a rush, propelled by a huge sweep of wind. The wind bursts into the room like a tornado, picking up letters on the table and my magazine and swirling them in frantic circles in the room. My hair blows up around my shoulders and head and my baggy sweater is lifted up at the bottom by the gust so my skin is chilled by the wet air. I hang on to Lily with all my strength, determined not to let her get whipped up, too.

The wind pounds at us both, and even through the tightness of my grip, I feel Lily being pulled from me. Her thin little body is sucked right out of my arms and sways up into the air, hovering above me, smiling even though she's precariously dangling there. A prize held up tantalizingly out of my reach.

"Lily, Lily. Come back to me, honey," I call, but the words are drowned by the sounds of the storm, which fill the room with their loudness. The walls reverberate with the pressure.

"No, please, come back, come back, sweetie. Come baaaaaack."

Lily stays there, still, in the air for a minute, then starts to drift to the end of the room and then toward the open door. Frantically, I rush after her, clawing at the gust, trying, trying to save her from the relentless gust. But it's no use.

Tears snake their way down my cold cheeks as Lily floats toward the open door and then right through it. The wind she coasts on seems smooth and airy, not like the frantic blowing we had endured moments ago.

I follow her outside, where the rain still batters against the beach and the water and the lighthouse walls. Instantly, I'm drenched but I don't even care. All I care about is retrieving Lily. She's floating ahead of me in the air and I trail behind, tired and wet and defeated, but unwilling to give up. I feel a rush of adrenaline sweep through me, urging me on to save her, to get her back, to hold her to me.

I chase after her desperately, my feet instantly plunged into wetness, and I realize that the beach has been swallowed up by the ocean. The solid base of the lighthouse has disappeared beneath high, white-crested waves. They dance and swish against the rocks and the wooden tower, sounding hard and angry. The flashing light from the tall porch casts shadows in the gurgling water and draws shapes and colors there, on the surface, that shift and change with each wave, creating new and different patterns, like a kaleidoscope turning.

Knee deep in the cold shock of the water I watch Lily float higher and higher above me, a white mist so sheer I can see the blackness of the night behind her.

"Lily, Lily," I call, crying harder now.

Standing there, reaching my hands up helplessly into the night, I feel the rain ease. Then there's a sudden stillness in the air. The wind stops in its place, and the ocean surface is suddenly smooth again. Nevertheless, Lily continues to move toward the sky, her body bobbing like a white balloon above the beach, moving always higher. It's hard to see in the darkness even with the flashes of light, but as she reaches the height of the light on the tower, I swear I see a halo and wings take shape on her.

She's become an angel.

This thought warms my wet and shivering body. I imagine that I can see her smile.

"Goodbye, mommy, goodbye," she says.

The words echo in the thickness of the moist air as I watch Lily, my angel, float up toward the clouds, which minutes ago were hard and black. Before my eyes, they soften and blend into white puffs and Lily merges there into the shimmery mass until I can no longer keep her shape separate. It's all one blur of white mist. Then I'm filled with a strange new peace that floats through my body and leaves me weightless. This feeling surprises me greatly. Yet I linger there for a minute yet, trying to see Lily one last time.

Then I give up.

I take one last look at the clouds and the sky. Then I say goodbye to Lily.

"Bye, darling. Take care, my Lily, my baby," I whisper, my voice thin and shaky. I know that I'll never see her again and although I'm saddened and a little empty at this thought, at the same time I'm also glad for her. I think that she's finally moved on to Heaven, which is where she belongs.

Finally, I go back to the lighthouse, which surprisingly stands there looking the same as it had before the storm, untouched by the havoc that the ocean and the beach—and I—have all undergone. I'm marveling over this fact when the truth hits me. Of course the lighthouse would be fine. With a flash of recognition similar to the flashes that come from the light tower, I suddenly know that the lighthouse just *had* to survive the night. This lighthouse has stood tall and brave for 250 years, guiding sailors through hundreds of severe storms, helping them find their way in the darkness.

Maybe I, in my grief, am like a sailor who's been lost at sea. The lighthouse has pulled me in to safety, too. My lighthouse, my beacon. It's illuminated things for me in a new way, although I'm much too tired to make much sense of all this tonight. But I'm sure that there's a lesson here somewhere. There must be.

Chapter 21

Very, very early the next day, when dawn is breaking over the island, filtering everything with a soft screen of light, I stand on the lighthouse bridge and survey the damage left from the night before. While the lighthouse appears new and shiny from the storm, the beach is dirty and tattered. Dried leaves from the trees that line the road have been swept all the way onto the sand and to the edge of the water, where they lie together with twigs and rocks and bits of debris. Red and green slivers of seaweed are clumped everywhere, with black algae and a scattering of shells and a few dead fish. The tide has receded quite a bit, but the water is still way too high and most of the sand is stained darker than usual from it.

Despite the mess, there's something pretty and vibrant about the scene and I think of how nice it would look captured on canvas. Even after all the storm's damage, the beach is filled with such light and movement and life, and every second it's changing slightly. I have such a desire to capture this motion and hold it in place. I haven't thought about my artwork in a long time, but today I embrace the unexpected desire to create something new, something beautiful in its own right.

I go inside to get a piece of paper and a pencil to sketch out my thoughts. With my supplies, I come back outside and stand on the porch again and lean my chin on my hand to study the play of the light on the water, seeing how it moves with the waves and dances there, rocking and rolling.

Then I feel like someone is watching me and I turn and cup my eyes with my hands, squinting into the early morning sunlight to see who's there. Someone's standing about 20 or 30 feet away, too far for me to make out the features but there's something to the stance that reminds me of Jim, and I hold my breath, hoping it will be him.

It *is* Jim, I realize seconds later, recognizing his jacket, which I had bought him last year for his birthday. When he sees me, he moves toward me quickly and I run to meet him, too. We cross the distance between us with easy steps, bridging not only the ground but the chasm, too.

I don't know who hugs the other first—everything is such a blur of arms and warmth and bodies pulling toward each other that it's hard to separate the motions—but I do know that I stand there in Jim's arms for a long, long time, savoring our reunion. And I think, again, of the day Jim and I met here and later fell in love. I wonder if he's recalling that day, too, and thinking about what it means for us now.

"I was so worried about you here alone," Jim says finally. He pulls out of my embrace but weaves his fingers through mine, letting me know in his way that he's still here, and is still very much with me. His touch seems warm and familiar, right.

"I *was* really scared," I tell him, grasping his arm tightly, wanting to hold him even closer to me. "But I'm fine now," I say, smiling at him. I can feel the smile flowing through me. I feel lighter than I've felt for a long time.

Jim tells me that he was afraid I'd be angry with him for disturbing my peace, but he was just so worried about me alone in the storm that he felt he had to come and check on me. He flew in on the first flight and took a taxi directly here from the airport.

"I'm really, really glad you did," I say. All the strain and awkwardness that lay heavy between us when I was home seems to have been washed away by the storm. This is

Jim again, here with me, not a stranger. I reach up and touch his arm, marveling that he made the trip to be with me. This is the Jim I fell in love with all those years ago, the one I always knew existed.

"I'm not mad, sweetie. Not at all," I say as I stroke Jim's arm. "I am so, so glad you're here. God, I really mean it. I am really glad to see you. I was scared last night, really scared. But now that you're here, I feel much better."

Jim leans against me and I'm bolstered by his weight resting against my arm and my leg, propping me up the way a bookend keeps a stack of books so firmly in place. It suddenly seems clear: we belong together.

I'm ready to leave the lighthouse and return to Boston with him and live in *our* apartment with all of *our* own things, not hiding in somebody else's space. I realize that while the lighthouse is a wonderful structure, it's Ida's place, not mine. My place is in Boston, beside my husband, a place that suddenly sounds very nice.

"I love you," Jim says impulsively, burying his lips against my neck. It's been a while since he's shaved. The stubble on his chin scrapes my tender skin and leaves rough marks that sting but also make me feel real and alive. Happy.

"I love you, too." I close my eyes and sink into the moment, letting the moistness of Jim's lips move up my chin to find my mouth and finally rest there, pressed against me as though we are frozen together.

Chapter 22

Was Lily truly there in the lighthouse with me? I suppose I'll never know for sure. She may have been a ghost that visited me, and then again, maybe she was just a figment of my grief-stricken imagination. How can one tell the difference when the whole thing feels like a dream? There's always the chance that over the years I had heard the story of the poor woman whose daughter had drowned on the lighthouse beach and maybe that idea of the little ghost lingered with me, causing me to imagine the same thing now, with the loss of my own baby. But who can tell?

The important thing is that I'm back in Boston now, back in my apartment as if I'd never left it. I'm back in my spot on the right side of the king-size bed, nearer to the bathroom and to the table with the alarm clock resting on it. And I'm back to making cinnamon toast and coffee in the mornings and sitting with Jim as we trade sections of the *Boston Globe* and eat our breakfast together. Then he leaves for work and I stay in the kitchen to work on my painting.

I've decided that maybe Jim was right after all when he wanted me to throw myself wholeheartedly into my artwork. Maybe the secret to healing from a tragedy does lie in focusing your energy on something else that fills you with passion and helps ease a bit of the emptiness. Ever since Lily's death, I've had this growing desire to create new life. But now I'm beginning to understand that beyond flesh and blood, there are other kinds of creations, too, that can spark my interest and give my life a focus and intensity along with it. While I know that one thing can't completely replace another, it does help me to embrace the days again and look forward to something fresh that has some of my character captured within it.

The project I'm working on now is a painting of the way the beach looked the morning after the storm. I'm trying to capture all the quivering layers of life that were hidden just below the surface. I'm not scheduled to return to teaching art classes at the school until next September, so I have a full nine months to focus on my own work. And my friends at the school tell me the new teacher, Sandy Gresson, is doing quite well with my class, so who knows. Perhaps I'll choose never to go back there and instead pursue my dreams of creating fine art full time.

My canvas sits on an easel in the kitchen and every so often I glance away from the evolving scene to see what's going on outside the window. This section of the city we live in is very pretty: the sidewalks are cobblestone and there are quaint gas streetlamps decked with Christmas wreaths on all the corners and windowboxes lining the street with colorful boughs of holly and other Christmas plants in them. At any time of day, you'll find throngs of people strolling through the neighborhood, their voices carrying in the crisp air right up the five stories and through my window.

As I watch today, I see an older couple pass by with their arms linked, faces turned toward one another, and there's something about them that reminds me of Ida and her late husband. I've been thinking about them a lot lately, wondering if Jim's and my relationship will evolve out of this tragedy into something more solid. I'm beginning to suspect so.

I used to find myself rushing at Jim constantly, trying to please him and keep the silences at bay. Now, though, when he comes home from work, I no longer rush to the door to greet him, helping him off with his coat and chatting to him about my day before he even has time to take a breath. Instead, I prefer to linger over my painting, concentrating on capturing the last bit of light before dusk falls. Jim can wait, and I know now that he will. I've learned that from my time away. And I've learned not to be so afraid of those periods when he needs to withdraw. If he's given the time and space to pull back and think things through when he feels emotionally threatened, I'm confident that the warmer side of Jim will, time after time, return to me and we'll be able to go on as always. After making it through the past two months, I now believe we can make it through anything together.

Tonight, I hear Jim enter the apartment and hang up his coat. He comes into the kitchen and watches me work. I'm filling in the lavender-and-white-edged shadow that rims the early morning sun, my hand moving almost without me, as though propelled of its own accord. And I think, without even realizing where I'm going with this, that it's Lily who is guiding me, helping me to see things more clearly.

I'm convinced that Lily's spirit lingers on. But with a new, sharp burst of clarity, I realize that it may not be in the same way that I had thought earlier. Then, I was looking for signs and physical evidence of her presence. But now I know that she's not in the wind or in the walls or in the grasses that surround the lighthouse. Now I know that she's everywhere, living on inside of me. This knowledge fills every inch of me with comfort.

I think Jim has come to a new acceptance of Lily's death, too.

"I want to show you something," he says tonight when we go into the bedroom.

"What is it?" I ask eagerly.

"It's sort of a surprise. You have to sit down and I'll get it."

Obediently, I sit on the edge of the bed and clasp my hands in my lap, waiting to see what it is. He ducks into our closet and rummages around, clanking and moving things, trying to find whatever it is. Finally he emerges, holding a small, pink stuffed bear in his hands, looking at me questioningly.

"Oh, Jim." I feel my breath catch in my chest. We had bought this toy for Lily last winter, high on excitement when we had first learned I was pregnant.

A few weeks ago, the sight of the bear would have completely unnerved me. But now I realize I can deal with this.

Jim tentatively holds the bear out to me—the pink fur fluffs out between his fingers and the new plush smell fills the room—and I reach out and take the animal into my own hands and gently cuddle with it.

"I couldn't give this away with the other things," he says somberly. "I wanted to keep something of Lily's for us to cherish."

His words strike a chord deep inside of me. I so clearly remember the day when we bought the bear at FAO Schwartz over on Boylston Street. The store had been filled with kids of all ages, faces open and eyes wide as they took in the vast and colorful assortment of wonderful toys. Jim and I had looked eagerly at the different features and hair and body types, wondering what our own child would look like.

The bear in my arms brings it all back in a rush and even as my eyes cloud at the thought, I find myself smiling at Jim.

"Thanks, honey," I say. "I'm really glad you kept this." We had bought the bear with such hope, and even though things didn't turn out the way we planned, a trace of that hope still lives inside me, refusing to be extinguished.

And as Jim turns out the light, I press closer to him, resting my hands on the tiny extra fold of skin still left from my pregnant stomach. Someday this space may fill again with new life. The possibility causes a stir in my chest, gently lifting a corner of the sadness that has been curtaining my heart since Lily's death.

Outside my window, the wind swirls, wrapping the city in its momentum. Back in the lighthouse, I would have heard Lily in its hum, would have found a way to use its power to bring her into my arms. Now, though, I know my baby is all spirit, no form. In her absence, I embrace Jim instead and use the wind as a means to send her my now-peaceful thoughts.

I like to think that Lily's essence lingers above, helping to open my mind, as well as my body, to whatever comes. Jim shifts in the cradle of my hug as if he can sense the relief that's beginning to flow through me. Some of the wrinkles in our marriage have been pressed smooth since I've been home, and I feel a wave of certainty that our relationship will continue to grow as the years unfold. I know, now, that whatever comes, we'll be strong enough to face it, cemented together forever by our memories of the everlasting day we shared with Lily.

CPSIA information can be obtained at www.ICGtesting.com
Printed in the USA
LVOW12s0232290514

387727LV00011B/116/P

9 781619 353671